Girls Only
The Complete Series

By Selena Kitt

eXcessica publishing

Girls Only Collection © 2014 by Selena Kitt

Excessica LLC
P.O. Box 127
Alpena MI 49707

To order additional copies of this book, contact:
books@excessicapublishing.com
www.excessica.com

Cover art © 2014 Willsin Rowe
First Edition Girls Only Collection July 2014

Table of Contents

New Year's Resolution

"Lose weight."

Beth snorted and pinched the side of Tina's trim thigh. "If you lose weight, you'll disappear, Tinkerbelle." Tina wiggled away from Beth's wandering fingers with a grin. "Think of something else."

"Stop smoking."

Beth laughed out loud at that. Tina hadn't ever smoked in her life. "Listen, princess, if you're not going to take this seriously, I'm going to have to tickle you again."

Tina squealed, grabbing for the covers and pulling them over her tousled blonde head. "No more tickling!"

"Then tell me honestly..." Beth's hand sneaked under the covers, seeking heat. "What's your New Year's resolution gonna be?"

Tina's eyes were bright as she peeked over the top of the comforter. "Okay, okay... you really want to know?"

Beth's hand had found the sweet spot she was searching for. The way Tina bit her lip when Beth slipped her fingers up and down in the wetness was both hot and endearing, and she felt her own body respond.

"I wouldn't have asked, if I didn't want to know, sweetness..." Beth flipped the comforter off in an instant, making Tina squeal again at the shock and pedal back toward the headboard. Beth's hands gripped the blonde woman's thighs and pulled her downward with no effort at all. Tina was tiny, a lightweight, and she could toss her around like a little ragdoll when she wanted to. It was one of the many things Beth loved.

"Ohhhh god," Tina wiggled and spread as Beth's probing fingers and tongue found their way past her soft, smooth lips and into the pink folds inside. "I can't think when you're doing that, baby."

Beth fastened her mouth over the tender, swollen bud of Tina's clit. Her flesh was incredibly responsive, and Beth knew in just a few moments time, she could bring the little blonde to a hard, quick orgasm. Tina's hips were already beginning to move against her tongue. Instead, Beth pulled back and grinned. "Well, in that case, I'll just stop until—"

"Nooooo!" Tina wailed, grabbing Beth's dark head and pressing her between her thighs. "Please, please..."

"Then tell me." Beth's tongue flicked back and forth, barely touching the woman's clit. "What's your New Year's resolution gonna be? I told you mine. It's only fair..."

Tina groaned, reaching down and spreading her lips with her fingers, rubbing her own clit. "I can't... tell... you..." She was making fast circles, her breath coming in short, hard pants.

"Ha!" Beth snatched the blonde's hand away from her pussy, wiggling herself between Tina's thighs and pressing her full, round breasts against Tina's mound. "You better tell... I swear, I'll tickle you again until you can't breathe!" Beth's fingers inched their way up Tina's sides and she squirmed, begging.

"No, no, no tickling!" Tina gasped and wiggled and Beth shivered as her nipples brushed through the slick wetness between Tina's thighs. "Okay, I'll tell you..."

With a satisfied smile, Beth kissed her way down Tina's smooth, flat belly, her eyes moving over the blonde's face, those sweet, delicate features twisted in pleasure as Beth began licking again. Tina moaned, rocking her hips up and down, her fingers twisting and tugging at her own little nipples, the pink flesh turning red with her attention.

"Oh yes!" Tina spread wide when Beth's fingers found her, slipping deep inside. "You know I love that..."

Beth did. Her fingers curled inside, seeking that sweet, sensitive spot and rubbing there, again and again. She loved watching Tina wiggle and squirm and moan under her mouth and fingers. There couldn't be anything better in the world.

"My New Year's resolution..." Tina gasped, her thighs trembling as she pulled them back to give Beth more room, deeper access. "Oh fuck, baby... please..."

Beth tried not to grin, but she couldn't help it as she flicked her tongue back and forth over that sensitive little clit. Tina's nails were digging into the soft flesh on the sides of her knees, making crescent shapes there as she rocked against Beth's mouth.

"Tell me," Beth urged, taking only a moment to say the words and then focusing again on the woman's clit, her fingers working hard inside, against the smooth walls of the little blonde's pussy.

"Oooooo baby!" Tina's whole body was quivering. "Make me come first, and then I'll tell you! Please!"

"You promise?" Beth's tongue pressed faster, harder, looking up into Tina's flushed face.

"Oh I promise!" she gasped, trembling with her longing. "Yes, yes, I promise, please! Make me come, oh baby, make me—"

There was no stopping it now. Tina quivered with her climax, one hand pressing Beth's dark head between her legs, the other rubbing hot, delicious friction over her nipple as she shuddered and bucked on the bed. Beth drank her in, swallowing the hot flood of her juices, thicker and more copious as she came and came into her waiting mouth.

"Oh god." Tina's knees fell open, like spreading angel's wings, and she threw an arm over her eyes. "You're so good to me, I can't stand it."

"You promised," Beth reminded, her fingers walking up the sensitive, ticklish expanse of Tina's ribs, making the blonde whimper.

"Okay, okay!" Tina peeked out from under her arm and bit her lip. "I'll tell you."

Beth waited, her fingertips drumming over Tina's ribcage, making her jump.

"My New Year's resolution..." Tina took a deep breath and said it quickly, as if she were trying to get it out as fast as possible. "Is to buy a strap-on and fuck you with it."

Beth's eyes widened and her heart lurched in her chest. "What?"

Rolling to her belly, Tina hid her flushed cheeks against the cool surface of the pillow. "I told you I couldn't tell you! I knew you'd be mad!"

Beth's fingers moved over the soft flesh of Tina's behind, kneading there. She smiled and pressed her lips there. "I'm not mad."

Glancing hesitantly over her shoulder, Tina's eyes narrowed. "You're not?"

"No." Beth grinned as she eased past the shock of it, feeling her own pussy quivering at the thought. "In fact... I think we should go shopping."

Tina's eyes widened then, a hint of a smile on her lips. "We should?"

Beth stood and stretched, reaching for her t-shirt. "Get up and get dressed. We're going to the toy store."

The blonde's eyes were stunned, her jaw open, but not working.

"Hurry up." Beth grinned. "Before I tickle you again."

That got Tina moving, and they both quickly dressed, the silence between them full of tingling anticipation.

* * * *

Beth shuddered as Tina held up a life-like dildo modeled after some male porn star. "You're not getting that thing anywhere near my cooch, girlie."

Tina giggled, waving it back and forth. "Come on... it's even got realistic balls!"

"Good, then I can kick them." Beth grimaced. "Put it back."

Tina put it back with the rest of the toy display with a sigh. "We're never going to find anything at this rate."

"Hey!" Beth edged over to the next aisle where several leather harnesses hung from hooks. "Now we're talking..."

Tina followed her, eyeing the thick straps. "Yeah. I can see myself strapping on one of these."

Beth's eyes gleamed. "So can I... damn, you'd look hot in this..." She lifted a leather harness and held it out in front of Tina's slim hips.

- 4 -

"You can try it on, if you want."

Both women jumped and whirled to face the guy who had moved in behind them. He was an older man with a salt and pepper beard, and he was wearing a name tag that said: "Ron" below the "Sexy Stuff" logo.

Beth blushed and blinked at him, quickly putting the harness back. "Oh, no. Thanks anyway."

Tina grinned. "Actually, do you have something fun for both the strap-on and the, uh, strap-ee?"

Ron smiled. "I sure do. Come this way."

Beth snapped the elastic of Tina's skirt as she passed, making a face at her, but Tina stuck her tongue out, following Ron around the corner. Beth sighed, reluctantly following. Walking into a sex toy shop took enough courage for her, but talking about toys in front of someone—a man, no less! That was too much.

"This one is nice, because it has a vibrating egg inside that's designed to stimulate the external genital area of the female wearer." Ron held up a black strap on with a large black dildo attached. Beth hid behind Tina, wincing as the blonde took the strap-on from the man and inspected it. "You can try it on if you like. We have a dressing room in back. For toys, we ask that you wear a pair of disposable panties we provide, of course, and please, no penetration."

Beth could feel her face burning. She was all about being the dominant one in the bedroom, but as far as she was concerned sex was private, and should be kept that way. They'd always argued about getting a strap-on, because while Beth wanted to order one via the Internet, Tina insisted they had to see and feel the merchandise. Now Beth had finally relented, and she was face-to-face with a man talking to them about the "external genital area of the female!"

"I want to try it on." Tina grinned over her shoulder at Beth. "Lead on, Ron... where's the dressing room?"

Inwardly, Beth groaned, but she followed them both toward the back of the store. Ron took a key off his belt and unlocked a dressing room door.

"There are disposable panties there, in those dispensers." He nodded toward the container on the wall. "Just let me know when you're through, or if you'd like to try something else. I can always get it for you."

Tina thanked him, pulling Beth into the cubicle and shutting the door behind them. Beth sank onto the bench, covering her eyes with her hands as Tina pulled a pair of panties out of the dispenser. They were wrapped in plastic, and she tore the wrapper eagerly with her teeth.

"This is so embarrassing." Beth whispered, glancing toward the door as if she were sure Ron was just on the other side, listening.

Tina grinned, kicking off her shoes. "You're cute when your cheeks are all red like that."

"Brat." Beth's hand came down on Tina's behind as the blonde pulled her skirt and panties off. "We're alone now, you know."

"I know." Tina put her foot up on the bench beside Beth and spread her smooth pussy lips, showing her girlfriend pink. Beth's eyes brightened and she leaned in to kiss Tina's exposed clit, making her squirm and sigh. "Gotta get these panties on."

"Very fashionable," Beth remarked, licking her lips, loving the taste of pussy in her mouth and throat as she swallowed. Tina pulled the thin, stretchable mesh panties on. "I assume those are one-size-fits-all or something?"

"Probably." Tina stretched the material way out in front of her taut, flat belly. "These would fit a pregnant woman!"

Beth fingered the leather straps of the strap-on and murmured, "This is sexy as hell."

Tina's eyes brightened. "I know. Put it on me."

Beth helped her with the straps, snapping and buckling them in place and pulling them taut. Tina stood in front of the mirror and wrapped her hand around the big, black cock, stroking it up and down the shaft. Beth bit her lip, watching, feeling her pussy responding to the sight of her girlfriend with leather straps across her hips and a huge dildo between her legs.

"Like it?" Tina's voice was husky as she met Beth's eyes in the mirror. Beth just nodded, swallowing hard as Tina pulled her t-shirt off, so that she was completely naked except for the strap-on and mesh panties. "How about now?"

"Fuck, baby!" Beth breathed, her hand pressing between her legs over the crotch of her jeans.

"Yeah." Tina's hips swayed as she came forward, pressing the black cock to Beth's lips. "I am... I'm gonna fuck you so good and hard..." Beth groaned, licking and sucking the head of the dildo, her eyes on her girlfriend's face. Tina smiled. "Play with yourself, baby. I want to watch."

Beth unsnapped and unzipped, wiggling her jeans and panties down her hips to her knees. Her pussy—just as smooth and soft as Tina's; they shaved each other every other day—was soaking wet and her fingers sank easily into her flesh.

"Think this thing has batteries?" Tina mused, searching for and finding the "on" switch. The vibrating egg between her legs began to hum and she gasped, her eyes half-closing in pleasure. "Ohhh yes... batteries included... thank God!"

Beth groaned around the shaft of the dildo as Tina's hips rocked, pressing the head of the cock deeper into her throat. Her clit was throbbing and she rubbed it in fast circles as Tina fucked her mouth.

"That feels so gooooood, baby," Tina moaned, rolling her hips as she pressed forward. Beth knew the vibrating egg was rubbing right against the blonde's clit through the disposable panties, and the harder she pressed, the better it felt. "God, I can't wait to fuck you with this big cock..."

Beth groaned, rubbing faster, her pussy on fire. She moved the cock around and around in her mouth, pressing back hard, making Tina gasp and squirm. The rocking motion was rubbing the little egg over and over Tina's sensitive clit, and she tugged hard at her nipples.

"Oh God, oh God," Tina whispered. "I'm gonna come, baby!"

Beth couldn't respond with the cock in her mouth, and she couldn't have, anyway, because she was coming, too, her mouth clamping down hard around the cock in her throat, her pussy rhythmically squeezing her own plunging fingers. Tina shuddered and arched, her hands on her hips, thrusting the big, black cock she was wearing deep into her girlfriend's mouth as she came, as if with every thrust, she was filling her with something.

When the knock came at the door, both women jumped and scrambled for their clothes, blushing furiously. "Ladies? Can I get you anything?"

"Thanks, Ron!" Tina called, tossing the disposable panties in the trash and pulling her clothes on. Beth snapped and zipped her jeans, her face flushed. Tina quickly wiped the saliva off the dildo and she opened the door a crack to see the man smiling knowingly through the opening. "You know what... we'll take it!"

* * * *

"I didn't realize it was so damned big!" Beth gasped, wincing as Tina edged the huge black cock between her slick pussy lips.

"Hold still!" Tina insisted, giving Beth's ass a slap and making her yelp.

"Hey!" Beth snorted, glancing over her shoulder at her girlfriend. "Who died and made you boss?"

"Seems to me, the boss is the wearer of the strap-on." Tina grinned, pressing her hips forward. Beth gasped as the dildo stretched her wide, sinking deep into her flesh.

"You brat!" Beth squirmed, gripping the sheet in both fits. "God damn, that thing is fucking huge!"

"I know." Tina pulled back and out, slapping the dildo against her girlfriend's ass. "I have a nice big cock to fuck you with."

"I'm starting to regret this New Year's resolution business," Beth grumbled as Tina slid the cockhead through her slit again, up and down.

"Awww, don't be like that." Tina wiggled the tip against Beth's clit, back and forth. "Give it a chance. I think you're going to like it."

"You keep saying that..." Beth murmured, arching back as Tina rubbed her pussy with the hard cock. It tickled her sensitive clit, back and forth, round and round, making her squirm for more.

"I promise..." Tina turned on the vibrating egg and the dildo vibrated a little too, making Beth moan softly and spread wider. "You're gonna like it, baby."

"I do like that," Beth gasped as Tina rocked the cock back and forth through her slit. "We could do that all day..."

"Rub your clit for me," Tina urged, easing back. Beth's fingers searched out her throbbing clit and made little circles there. "Does that feel good?"

"Mmmm..." Beth wiggled and arched, rubbing faster.

"Don't stop." Tina aimed the cock, attached around her hips with leather straps, and thrust. Beth groaned, but she didn't stop touching herself. The thick black cock eased her open inch by inch and Tina pressed forward until she felt resistance.

Beth felt the vibration of the egg all the way through the shaft of the dildo as Tina began to rock, fucking her slowly. Tina's thumbs kneaded the flesh of her ass, opening her up further with the motion. Beth's fingers rubbed faster and faster, her clit aching.

"How's that, baby?" Tina gasped, thrusting in and out, a little faster now. "Is that good?"

Biting her lip, Beth pressed her cheek to the sheet, which arched her back even further, pushing the cock deeper. Tina's silky thighs brushed hers with every thrust.

She didn't want to admit it, but it felt incredible! The dildo opened her wide, sinking deep into her flesh with every pass.

"Oh god!" Tina moaned. "Your pussy is so gorgeous... you should see this cock fucking your hot little hole..."

Beth moaned, too, her clit like a thick pulse under her fingers. She was so close to coming her whole body was trembling with it. Tina thrust faster, her hips rocking and her breath coming in short pants. Her thumbs rubbed Beth's ass, working inward until she was massaging around her tight little asshole.

"What are you doing?" Beth wiggled and squirmed, moaning.

"Feel good?" Tina's finger pressed the little rosebud hole, massaging around and around. "It's so tight. Maybe I'll fuck you there, next."

Beth startled at the thought, but her pussy throbbed in response. "Oh God..." Her voice was a low growl, her back arching. "Ohhh fuck, baby, make me come all over that big, fat dick!"

That did it for both of them. Tina made a low noise in her throat as she bucked up against Beth's shuddering ass. They came together, Tina's finger slipping into Beth's ass and wiggling there, sending extra waves of pleasure through them both. Beth eased forward, the cock slipping out of her pussy, and she rolled over to smile at her girlfriend.

"Here." Tina eased herself over Beth, straddling her chest. "Lick it."

Beth did, sucking and licking her own juices off the thick end.

Tina watched, her eyes bright, easing the cock a little further into Beth's mouth. "That was so fucking hot."

"Especially when you put your finger in my ass," Beth murmured, licking up the shaft.

Her eyes brightened and Tina smiled. "You liked that, huh?"

Beth nodded, reaching under the dildo to press her hand to Tina's mound, making her shiver. "Yeah... a lot."

"Well then... maybe next time, I'll put that big black cock in your ass." Tina grinned.

Beth pressed the vibrating egg hard against Tina's pussy and grinned back. "Promises, promises."

"Not a promise... a *resolution.*"

Beth leaned in to kiss her. "I love your resolve."

Sybian Sorority

I didn't want to pledge. When my mother suggested I check out her Greek alma mater, I told her smugly, I'd rather cut off my left arm than walk through the doors of some stuck-up sorority.

But that was all before I met Chloe.

"It's just a meeting!" My new roommate was both alluring and persuasive, but if it weren't for the instant click that happened when we met, I wouldn't have even considered it.

"I'm not the type," I grumbled, lamenting that my new Kindle, where all my textbooks were currently downloaded, wasn't big enough for me to really hide behind—but I tried.

Chloe pouted. I hadn't yet been subject to the full force of the Chloe pout, and the pushed-out lower lip and big, sad brown eyes were almost enough to melt my resolve. Almost. But then she spoke.

"I don't want to do it without you." Her voice actually quivered. I swear to god. I pretended not to notice. "It won't be any fun if you don't come."

I made my voice cheerful and light. "Sure it will! You'll have a blast, Chlo. Go for it!"

She sighed, sitting on her bed, across from mine, and stared at the floor. "Never mind then."

Great.

I flipped through the menu on my Kindle, looking for my physical science textbook—we had two chapters to read before Monday. I needed something to do besides trying not to look at Chloe tracing flower patterns on her bedspread. She actually looked like she was about to cry.

Christ.

"Look, do you know the crow I'd have to eat if I joined a sorority?" I sat up, tossing my Kindle on the bed. "I told everyone how much I hate them—my mother, my sister—there's no way I can pledge. No way."

"That's okay." She sighed, blinking fast and looking toward the window, like there was something interesting there. She had a habit of twirling a long strand of blonde hair around and around her finger. "You don't have to."

I took a deep breath and tried a different angle. "I'm really not the sorority type. I mean—look at me!" I held my arms out, glancing down at my baggy black sweater and jeans. "I'm a brainiac. I practically have to wear my glasses to bed. I can barely wear a one-piece, let alone a bikini." I pulled at the short, dark curly mop on top of my head that liked to masquerade as hair. "I'm not even blonde, for Christ's sake!"

"Oh, Violet." Chloe rolled her eyes. "It's so not like that. You'll make lots of friends—and trust me, there are tons of smart girls. You have to have and maintain a 3.0 GPA to get in!"

I frowned and cocked my head at her. "You do?"

She nodded, sensing my give, and edged a little closer, leaning forward as she talked. The fact that her v-neck blouse dipped to show her not inconsiderable cleavage didn't hurt either. "There's nothing like the sisterhood. I promise you, it'll be something you'll always remember."

"Right." I sighed, trying to keep my gaze away from the swell of her breasts. "Because of the abject humiliation and degradation they put me through before I join?"

Chloe laughed, letting the strand of hair she'd been playing with unravel into a long, blonde curl. "Is that what you're worried about? They don't do hazing anymore. It's not allowed."

I snorted. "That's what they tell you just before they make you strip naked and moon Gamma Delta Whatever."

"Well..." She lowered her voice conspiratorially, eyes bright. "I've got it on good authority that the hazing at Eta Nu Pi isn't bad. In fact, it's quite fun."

"Fun?" I snorted. "I very much doubt that."

"Come on, Violet." She gave me the puppy dog eyes again, and this time I wasn't distracted. Damn, she was tough to say no to. "Please? For me? Just come to the meeting. If you hate it, we'll leave. I'll go with you. I promise."

I sighed, glancing at the clock. "Oh hell. Why not? I didn't want to read about transition metals, anyway."

"Yay!" Chloe jumped up and actually clapped her hands in glee. "Let's go—before you change your mind!"

"Okay, okay!" I barely had time to grab my jacket—this fall in New England had been colder than usual—before she yanked me out the door.

* * * *

The girls were normal. They weren't all cheerleader-types, or even all blonde. There were quite a few who were even less style-conscious than me, surprisingly enough, and Chloe was right about the requirements, including maintaining a 3.0 GPA. I was also impressed with their service record—they volunteered at shelters, did fundraisers for UNICEF, and each girl had a special pet cause she brought to the group. Chloe gave me "I told you so" eyes all night.

"Well, there's still no shortage of parties and beer bashes, looks like," I mumbled, pulling out the "social events calendar."

"A girl's gotta have fun," Chloe whispered back, nudging me as the girl talking—a lanky, dark-haired thing whose glasses were, sadly, even thicker than mine—noticed our tête-à-tête and looked our way.

"Are there any questions?" The girl with the glasses looked directly at both of us.

I raised my hand and starting speaking before she even called on me. "Is there any hazing involved?"

The glasses-girl—Julie, that was her name, written in loopy script on her name tag and barely visible to me from this distance—cleared her throat and looked at another girl sitting next to her. That one was blonde, cute and perky, but she looked smart too. Her name tag said Megan. It was the blonde who stood and spoke. "Hazing is traditional in a lot of fraternities and sororities. I can promise you, though, you won't have to do anything you don't want to do."

Julie took someone else's inquiry and I raised an eyebrow as Chloe leaned in to whisper, "That really didn't answer my question, did it?"

"Don't worry." Chloe reached over and squeezed my fingers in hers. "I'll protect you."

I snorted, leaning back on the couch with a roll of my eyes. I couldn't believe I was doing this. It was so out-of-character for me I thought maybe I was going schizo or something. Chloe smiled over her shoulder at me, and I could tell she was gauging my reaction, or trying to. She looked nervous, like she wasn't sure I was liking it. And I wasn't sure myself. Okay, so she wanted to join a sorority, and she wanted me to join with her. What was so wrong with that?

I mean, besides the fact I'd never been one to hang out with the popular crowd, and for me, the word "sister" meant someone who stole my makeup, tattled, and liked to tag along everywhere I went. What would it be like to be a part of a whole group of women, bonded together, in some sort of secret sisterhood? Part of me said it was creepy and cult-like, and I shouldn't even consider it. But another part of me—the part that watched Chloe when she stood in her bra and panties in front of our mirror and brushed her long blonde hair every night—thought it might be interesting. Maybe more than just a little interesting.

And if it gave me more of an opportunity to be with her, what was the harm? I knew I wasn't brave enough to tell her the truth—I hadn't told anyone. I had barely admitted it to myself. I'd kept up the pretenses as well as I could. I'd even gone to my senior prom with a boy from my Algebra II class—although I'd rebuffed all of his drunken advances afterward. But if the few experimentations and secret flings I'd had with girls in high school had been crushes, this thing I had for Chloe went far beyond infatuation.

I touched Chloe's shoulder, getting her attention, and she turned to me with curious eyes. Smiling, I leaned in to whisper in her ear. "Hey, let's pledge, whatdya say?"

She brightened. "You mean it!?"

I cringed when the whole room turned at her squeal. "Yeah, I mean it."

I had no idea what I was getting into.

* * * *

"Where are we going?" Chloe's hand in mine was warm and slightly damp. I tried to squeeze it reassuringly but I wasn't quite sure myself. The girl in front of me had a death grip on my other hand as we made our way blindfolded down a flight of stairs and I stumbled, threatening to topple the whole chain of girls.

"Careful!" the girl in front of me hissed, her hand tightening to bone-crushing levels.

"I told you a sorority was a bad idea," I whispered back to Chloe, experiencing a sudden temperature change as we came to the bottom of the stairs and inched our way into a more wide-open space. The basement of the sorority house, I realized. Had to be.

Chloe whispered back, "I'm beginning to think you were right."

"Keep following the girl in front of you!" The instructions came from Megan, the blonde who had been leading us through everything that week, from the instruction about all of the sorority history to learning the secret handshakes and passwords. They were big on secrets, apparently, but all of it had been pretty harmless, even the whole not being allowed to shave our legs for the whole week stunt.

Thank god that one was over. Just this afternoon, right after lunch, Chloe and I had splurged on a Gillette Venus and some of that Pure Silk shaving cream for the occasion, going into shower stalls right next to each other to take care of business. We'd gone a little overboard though. Chloe had dared me to shave *everything,* and I'd told her I would if she would—and so we had.

I'd made an off-hand remark, trying to keep up pretenses, "Too bad neither of us has a boyfriend—I hear boys love it smooth like this." Chloe had laughed breezily, teasing me to distraction with her comment. "Who needs boys anyway?" The whole thing left me breathless with wonder, and now I was walking around all smooth and soft, feeling like a ten-year-old girl, the seam of my jeans constantly riding up my crotch, sending little shivers through me at the most inconvenient times.

"Ok, stop!" Megan commanded. "Face front and let go of each other's hands."

Doing this blindfolded was scary to say the least, but I could hear Chloe breathing beside me—a little too fast and hard. It wasn't from our trek down the stairs either, I was sure. It was from anxiety. I was a little freaked out too.

"Each of you has a senior sorority sister behind you for support," Megan said, and I felt a presence behind me. I was wondering just what this was all about. "No matter what you choose."

Choose? What did we have to choose?

"Now, strip." Megan's words hung in the air and I heard several of the girls gasp out loud. "You can choose not to. If you don't want to strip, raise your hand, and a sister will come remove you from the room."

I was about to raise my hand when she went on. "Of course, if you choose not to, you won't be part of Eta Nu Pi."

"Stay." Chloe grabbed for my hand, finding my wrist first, squeezing hard. "Stay with me."

She was really going to take her clothes off? "You're going to do it?"

I felt her answer—she let go of my hand and I heard her stripping off her t-shirt, felt the brush of the material against my arm as she dropped it to the floor.

"You decide," Megan reminded us in a loud voice. "Stay and strip—or leave."

Crap.

Chloe nudged me, whispering, "Please?"

There were girls leaving. I could hear them passing through the door to my left. I wondered how many pledges we were going to lose during this little stunt.

Reluctantly, I grabbed the edge of my t-shirt, pulling it off and dropping it to the floor. *All of the pledges were blindfolded anyway,* I told myself. What did it matter? But as I shoved my jeans down my hips, I was sure my mother and sister had never had to do anything like this to join a sorority.

"Everything, ladies!" Megan passed close to me as she said it and I nearly jumped back in surprise. "All your clothes off, but leave your blindfolds on!"

"This is crazy," I whispered, and I heard other girls whispering similar things. And it was—but we were all doing it. Or, many of us were.

"Now, when I tell you to take off your blindfolds, you're going to have another choice to make."

Oh great.

Chloe grabbed for my hand again and it really sank in that she was standing beside me naked. As roommates, we'd gotten glimpses of each other while we were changing, but I'd never really seen anything exciting. The thought of seeing her fully unclothed made my mouth go dry. I was going to have to try hard not to stare.

"Take off your blindfolds."

I slid it down around my neck, blinking at the fluorescents overhead, seeing the pledges I'd spent the week with standing in a circle around me, all of us completely nude. I wanted to look away, but there was nowhere else to look—except the middle of the room, where Julie was kneeling on a mat on the floor in front of some sort of black, rounded half-moon machine. It looked like it was made of the same material the mat was made of. It had a long cord that trailed out of the circle of girls to plug into the wall. But I didn't really pay much attention to that, because Julie herself was completely nude, just like we were.

What in the hell was going on?

"What is that thing?" I whispered to Chloe, but Megan was already answering my question—and I had forgotten all about not staring at my naked roommate. Her skin was still tanned from the summer, her tawny limbs long and shapely, her breasts lighter in color with a defined, triangle tan line, both of them cherry tipped. I glanced down and saw that she had kept her word—her pussy was completely shaved. But now I was even more curious—was the hair there naturally light or dark? The question tormented me.

"This is a Sybian, and Julie is going to demonstrate for us what it does in a minute." Megan smiled as Julie took out what couldn't be mistaken for anything but a cock, although it was a little shorter and not quite as defined as an actual dildo. It also had a fleshy colored pad attached with little nubs on it. I stared as she hooked it up to the machine. "You'll have a choice tonight—ride the Sybian or..." She held up a Ziploc bag but I couldn't tell from this distance what was inside. "Or take ecstasy."

I felt Chloe stiffen beside me. She was the most anti-drug person I'd ever met, probably because her older brother had overdosed on heroin when she was just ten or eleven. If she had to make a choice, I knew for sure she'd choose the Sybian. But what in the hell was the thing, and what did it do?

"And the ecstasy is just going to make you want to ride the Sybian anyway!" Julie giggled, sliding forward toward the machine she'd just attached the cock onto.

"No way," I breathed, but yes, it was really happening. Julie had a great body she'd been covering up with sweaters and bulky, long skirts. Her breasts were huge and heavy, her nipples and areolas dark. Her pussy hair was thick, and I couldn't help staring as she spread her lips and inched forward toward the dildo attached to the machine.

"Do it," Megan said, licking her lips. The pledges in the circle had forgotten about trying to cover themselves. We were all too stunned, staring as Julie slid down onto the cock. Now I understood the purpose of the flesh-colored pad underneath with all the ridges as Julie began rocking back and forth. Those little nubs rubbed her clit every time she moved.

"Ohhh god that's so good." Julie bit her lip and moved her hips faster, reaching forward and grabbing a little box.

"These are the controls," Megan explained as Julie used a dial on the remote and a distinct, low hum filled the room. "It vibrates."

I had figured that much out, just from Julie's moans, the way her head went back as soon as the sound started, her eyes closing in pure pleasure.

"And the cock," Julie gasped, opening her eyes and glancing up at Megan. "It... ohhhh! It rotates...inside... oh god!"

"It feels *really* good." Megan grinned, still walking around the circle. She sounded like she was talking from personal experience. "But more importantly, you're going to bare everything to your sisters. After tonight, you'll never look at each other in the same way again."

That was for damned sure, I thought, glancing over at Chloe, seeing her nipples were hard, the skin around them pursed. Most of the pledges were too stunned to react, and we were all enthralled by the sight of Julie rocking on the Sybian. Out of the corner of my eye, I noticed the girl to my right, the one I'd followed down the stairs, had her hand between her legs. Her fingers were moving between her pussy lips, playing in the dark, wiry hair there.

My own pussy ached in response and I longed to do the same, but I couldn't. Not in front of Chloe. Besides, she'd reached for my hand, clenching it hard as we watched Julie moaning on the Sybian. She was really riding it, her glasses sliding down her nose, her hair falling in her face. There was a matching black, padded block, like a stool, in front of the Sybian that she used to lean on for support, and she clearly needed it—her whole body was turning to Jell-O.

"Ohhhhh fuck!" Julie cried, throwing her head back, her mouth drawn into a perfect "O." And then she was coming. We all knew what it looked like, what it sounded like, the rising hum of the Sybian competing with Julie's moans of pleasure. I felt Chloe's nails digging into my hand as we watched our soon-to-be-sorority sister climaxing right in front of our eyes.

"I'm not riding that thing," protested one of the pledges. She was a chubby redhead named Kate. I noticed she was one of the few who hadn't stopped trying to hide herself, although it was impossible to really cover anything with just your hands, I'd discovered. Her lower lip was trembling. "It's unsanitary!"

Megan scoffed, opening up the trunk at the other side of the mat. "We have more attachments."

"And we sterilize them," Julie added, panting out the words, still out of breath as she turned off the Sybian and climbed down. The dildo was still wet with her pussy juices, glistening in the light.

"We can go if you want to." Chloe leaned in to whisper this to me.

"No, Chloe, this is important to you," I reminded her. I couldn't believe I was saying it, but I couldn't help myself. It was the thought of seeing Chloe naked and riding that thing that did it for me. "I think we should do it."

She stared at me, wide-eyed. "You do?"

"Do you want me to go first?" I gulped and held my breath. What in the hell was I thinking?

Then Chloe grinned, that mischievous look in her eyes. "I will if you will."

It reminded me of our little shower-bet, how we'd shaved down to nothing on a whim—how excited I'd been, knowing she was shaving her pussy at the same time as me. How I'd gone into a bathroom stall afterward and rubbed myself off to a mind-blowing orgasm just thinking about it.

I raised my hand. "I'll do it."

I think the whole room gasped.

"Well come on, girl!" Megan grinned, leading me over to the machine. The floor in the sorority basement was carpeted, and I padded over in bare feet, standing next to the Sybian while one of the sorority sisters switched out the accessories, handing the other over to be sterilized. She seemed very familiar with it. I stared at the fleshy-colored dildo and then glanced back at Chloe. She was watching me with those big, brown eyes, chewing on her lower lip, which she always did when she was nervous.

All eyes were on me.

"Climb on up." Julie was recovered now and she had a robe on. All the older sorority sisters were dressed—it was just the pledges who were naked. Julie patted the side of Sybian like it was a horse. "You won't regret it."

"Like this?" I hesitated, straddling the machine, but there was a girl on either side, helping me, showing me, and before I knew it, the dildo was inside of me and I was settled on the Sybian.

"Now comes the fun part." Megan moved in front of me, handing me the controls. "This one controls the vibration. And this one controls the rotation."

"The... rotation?" I raised my eyebrows, taking the box as she turned the rotation dial up. I gasped in surprise, feeling the dildo inside of me starting to turn. "Oh my God!"

"What is it?" Chloe called from behind me.

"Oh! My! God!" I cried out as Megan turned the vibration dial up.

"Violet!" Chloe moved to my side, surprising everyone, including me. I glanced up at her, reaching a hand out, and she took mine, her eyes wide. "Are you okay?"

I nodded. "It just... oh!... it just feels soooo good!"

"Really?" Chloe breathed, kneeling down beside me to stare between my legs, fascinated. Under other circumstances, I would have been mortified, but I was so surprised by the sensation that I actually leaned back a little so she could get a better look.

"It's, like, turning around... inside me." I tried to explain, but my hips were moving all on their own, those ridges rubbing right against my clit. It was so good, I could barely stand it. It was nothing like getting fucked by a man—there was no grunting and thrusting and plunging. This thing was like a lesbian's dream, doing things inside of me I couldn't have imagined, paying extra special attention to my aching clit.

"You are going to be so glad we shaved," I gasped, clasping onto Chloe's arm, trying to keep my balance. She giggled, grabbing onto me, her full breasts pressed against my side, her hair tickling my nose. I wanted to touch her—*really* touch her—but I didn't dare.

"It feels good?" she whispered.

I moaned, nodding, not able to say much. My nipples were hard and standing straight up, practically pointing toward the ceiling, my pussy so wet I could hear a squelching sound as I rode the machine, back and forth, round and round, so lost in pleasure I forgot all about the room of girls watching me get myself off. And they were all watching, most of them touching themselves, their heavy breath leaving the room humid and thick with feminine scent.

But I couldn't concentrate on that. I forgot it all, the girls, the sorority, the fact I was naked and getting fucked in front of everyone. I forgot about everything except Chloe and the glorious machine I was riding, the swelling sensation between my legs rising, making me quiver with longing.

"Oh God." I threw my head back, my whole body trembling with my impending climax. It was coming, and it was going to be epic. The rotation of the dildo inside of me increased and the vibration intensified. My eyes flew open in surprise and I looked over to see Chloe with the box, turning the controls on the dials. "Oh! Oh! Yes! Chloe! Oh my fucking god, I'm going to come so hard!"

Her eyes were bright and she licked her lips as she watched me bucking and moaning on the machine, my hips rocking, fucking it as fast and hard as I could. I shuddered and grabbed onto the stool in front of me, gripping the edges and biting my lower lip to keep from actually screaming out loud.

But I couldn't help moaning, the sound low in my throat, as my orgasm finally overtook me. I rubbed my clit fast against the ecstatic hum between my legs, feeling my juices running down the machine, my thighs wet with it. And the sensation didn't stop. The dildo inside of me kept turning, relentless, sending me flying so far into orbit I was sure I would never come down.

"Stop!" I managed to gasp out, reaching for Chloe's hand where she was holding the remote. "Ohhhh fuck! Stop, please, god, stop, or I'm going to die!"

Slowly, the vibration decreased, the rotation slowing, and I sat up, still shivering, panting, peeling dark, wet curls off my sweaty forehead. I'd made a mess of the machine, far more than Julie had. I could feel the wetness between my legs.

"Does it feel as good as it looks?" Chloe blinked at me.

"Try it and find out." I grinned as I slowly climbed off, practically collapsing onto the mat beside it. "It's your turn, right?"

"You want to go next, Chloe?" Megan asked. I looked up at her, feeling my face flush. I'd forgotten she was even here. I'd forgotten they were all here.

"Me next!" The chubby redhead rushed forward.

"No, me!" The dark-haired girl who had been standing in line next to me came forward too.

"Girls, girls!" Megan laughed. "We'll all get a turn. But you can come closer to watch if you want. Come on, don't be shy."

She waved the rest of the circle toward us, and they all ventured in bit by bit. The mat was large enough for most of them to kneel on it and they did. For a minute I thought I was dreaming, looking around at a room full of naked girls surrounding me.

"Wait!" Julie cried. I turned to see Chloe straddling the machine, grabbing onto the dildo. "We have to—"

It was too late. She was sliding it inside of her, already moaning.

"...sterilize...it..." Megan finished.

"I don't care! It's just Violet," Chloe gasped, reaching out for my hand. "Hold onto me."

I slipped my arm around her waist. She was a tall girl, far taller than me, her limbs long and tanned, and sitting astride the Sybian made her even taller. Kneeling up beside her on the mat, I found myself face to face with her breasts and their hard, pink, kissable nipples.

"Oh my god!" Chloe cried, turning the dials on the remote. She was far more proactive than I had been, taking charge right away. "What *is* this thing?"

"Heaven," I murmured, watching her hips begin to rock. She had the prettiest little pussy, newly shaved, her lips swollen around the dildo. I wanted to get down there and look close, even put my tongue there. Oh god, I wanted to taste her. "Isn't it good?"

"Yes! Ohhhh yesss!" She bit her lip and clung to me, wrapping her long arms around my neck as she rode the machine. She'd gone for broke, turning everything up to the highest setting and tossing the remote aside. Her eyes closed, her legs began to tremble, and I watched, fascinated, as she chased her orgasm, faster and faster, riding the Sybian like a pro.

"Gonna come!" she panted, pulling me close, closer, mashing my face against her breasts, the smell of her perfume filling my head, her hair curtaining us both as she came in my arms. I felt her body relax and she collapsed against me, letting me hold her up. She was almost sobbing with pleasure, the machine still going, going, going between her legs. "Ohhhh fuck! Violet! I'm gonna do it again!"

And she did, her body bucking, hips rolling, back arching, taking me with her, oblivious to everyone around us, every girl watching now, all of them with wet fingers, their nipples hard and pointing in our direction. I held her tight, whispering her name again and again, trying to call her back. Megan grabbed the remote, turning the Sybian down and then off.

"Violet." Chloe's eyes fluttered open and she smiled dreamily at me. "I want to do it again."

"Don't worry, we have Sybian parties once a month." Megan laughed and winked knowingly at me. *"No boys allowed."*

So she knew. How?

"Finally." Chloe reached for me, climbing off the machine and into my arms. I stared at her, wide-eyed with surprise, and she laughed. "Oh Violet, for someone who's so smart, sometimes you can be so stupid. I've wanted you since the day I met you."

"You...what?" That was all I managed before we were kissing, her mouth soft and open and hungry, her full breasts pressed to mine. Someone else was climbing up onto the Sybian—the chubby little redhead, I think, grabbing a newly sterilized toy—but Chloe and I were too involved to pay attention, kissing and touching and rubbing against each other on the mat, making it slick with our juices and our sweat.

"Oh! Oh! I'm gonna come!" The redhead cried out, and I broke our kiss to glance up and see her, mouth open, head back, her whole body vibrating with her orgasm.

"I knew about it." Chloe's whisper stilled the breath in my throat. "I knew all about the Sybian. I knew, if I just got you here... "

I looked around the room, stunned to see girls paired off like we were, kissing each other, touching, waiting eagerly for their turn on the Sybian.

"What is this?" I whispered, shivering as Chloe's fingertips grazed my nipple before she fully cupped my breast in her hand.

"Eta Nu Pi is a *real* sisterhood," she whispered back. "In every sense of the word."

I grinned. "I think I'm going to like being in a sorority."

"Me too," she whispered, kissing me on the lips, and for the second time that night, I forgot all about everyone else but her.

The Hairdresser

"Sorry I'm late!" I apologized as the door closed behind me, leaving the rain outside.

Jen looked up and smiled. She was sitting in her stylist chair, reading *People* and drinking something from a tall Starbucks cup. They were just around the corner and I had my own, picked up on the way. I glanced around the normally busy salon at the empty chairs and quiet dryers.

"We close in fifteen minutes," she admonished, already standing and beckoning me over. "So what do you have in mind, Mandy? Just a cut?"

"It'll be quick, I promise." I fingered the ends of my auburn hair, looking for split-ends. "Just a trim."

She patted the chair. "Hop up."

I stashed my purse under her table and slid onto the seat, smoothing my skirt and watching in the mirror as she fastened the black drape around my neck like a reverse Dracula's cape. Jen ran her hand through my hair, still thick although I was nearing thirty-five. My mother had started losing her hair at forty and I was paranoid about compromising my best feature.

"Half an inch? An inch?"

I nodded. "Sounds about right."

Pleasantries over, Jen got down to business, hustling me over to the sink to wash my hair before the cut. This was my favorite part of going to a salon—the warm water, the gentle scrubbing of her fingertips over my scalp, the press of her hip against my shoulder, and the lovely view of her cleavage as she bent to rinse the soap out.

Yes, I had a boyfriend—if you could call him that—but I couldn't help my sexual proclivities, such as they were. I'd always had a thing for pretty girls, although I'd learned not to confess this fact too often, especially to my male partners. They just wanted to talk about and push threesomes, and who wanted a guy breathing over you while you were trying to enjoy yourself with a girl?

Of course, I didn't tell women about it either, most of the time. In spite of what they told their boyfriends in college, most girls weren't really into other girls, especially if the attention of a guy wasn't at stake. So I just enjoyed their company and my own little secret, later fantasizing about it in the shower or in the middle of the night while Tom snored away next to me in bed.

The experience of Jen washing my hair was so pleasurable I often lost track of whatever small talk we were making at the time, and today's topic of conversation was so oft-traveled, I'm afraid my mind definitely wandered down the front of her blouse. She was complaining about her own on-again, off-again boyfriend, a bodybuilder named Brad who worked out four hours a day and liked mirrors more than his hairdresser girlfriend.

"Why do we bother with these bastards, Jen?" I met her eyes, shaking my head in disgust as she toweled my hair dry.

"You got me." She rolled her pretty blue eyes up under her thick, blonde bangs. Like most hairdressers, she was perfectly coiffed, her hair thicker and blonder then any Rapunzel. I could smell it when she leaned in close, fruity and sweet, and I caught another secret scent, the musky smell of her sweat and deodorant mixed. "Oh sweetie... what do we have here?"

"Hm?" I inquired, enjoying the way she dried me off like a naughty puppy after a bath too much to really take notice of her frown.

"A grey hair."

I stared at her, horrified, disbelieving, until she plucked it from my temple, the sharp sting making me yelp, my eyes watering.

"Ouch!" I stared at the hair pressed between her finger and thumb. It was grey all right. "You're not supposed to pluck them! Doesn't that make them come back even more?"

"That's an old-wives'-tale." She laughed. "Is it really your first?"

I gulped and nodded, to aghast to speak.

"You should keep it."

She found a perfume card in the middle of a magazine, black with small white lettering. Using Scotch-tape, she fastened my first grey hair to it in stark contrast.

"Keep it?" I scoffed as she walked me back over to her station, putting the card in front of me on the table as I sat down again. What for?"

"It's a sign of wisdom." She picked up a comb and started working it through my hair. "And it isn't the end of the world, you know."

"Look who's talking!" Now it was my turn to roll my eyes. "What are you, twenty?"

"Thirty." She smiled and tipped me a wink. "And this isn't my natural color."

"Oh my god, I'm old." I frowned into the mirror, too focused on my own face to notice her hair color. "Where did these lines come from?"

Jen turned my chair away from my reflection, leaning in so I couldn't look anywhere but her bright blue eyes. "You won't turn into a crone overnight, I promise."

"But it's the beginning of the end," I protested. Since I didn't have a mirror to point to, I showed her direct proof. "Look at my hands! Old, I tell you! I'm old!"

She pressed her lips together, arms akimbo, and then smiled, a slow, sweet smile. "I have an idea. Let's do a whole beauty regimen. Hair, nails, skin, everything."

I blinked in surprise. "Weren't you getting ready to close?"

"So? I'm the only one here and Brad's in Chicago at some bodybuilding conference for the weekend."

I looked at her, contemplative. "Funny, Tom's away on business this week. He won't be back until tomorrow night."

Jen smiled. "So it's just us girls."

"Guess so." I glanced back at the mirror, seeing her looking at me. "No one to get all prettied up for."

"Do it for you." She ran a hand through my wet hair, her fingers grazing my scalp lightly, giving me shivers.

I shrugged and then grinned. "Why not?"

We spent two hours dying, washing, drying, brushing and coiffing. We also spent that time talking, like we usually did, about everything from my job in graphic design to hers. She was also going to school part-time to get her degree in nursing.

We also talked about our boyfriends, both of us unhappy but unwilling to make a big change either. Tom had cheated on me—twice—and Jen had let me cry on her shoulder in both instances. But I'd still gone back to him. And Jen's boyfriend, Brad...well, I didn't tell her so, but I wasn't sure the man didn't swing the other way. He was too pretty for his own good. She complained about him going out to bars a lot. It just made me suspicious.

When my hair was done and my facial and make-up complete, the last thing we did was my nails, sitting across the little table from each other, heads bent and focused.

Jen sat back and studied her work, giving a satisfied nod. "Pretty."

"We should do you too."

She looked up and smiled. "I've got a better idea."

"Hmm?"

Jen leaned forward, so close I could smell the cappuccino on her breath. "Let's make it a real girl's night. Want to come back to my place? I've got a bottle of White Zinfandel we can share."

The offer was innocent enough, but the look on her face gave me a funny feeling in the pit of my stomach. I had a feeling that wasn't all we were going to share, and I turned out to be right. We polished off the entire bottle of wine sitting on Jen's bed, going through some of her old photo albums. I'd expressed an interest and had overruled her reluctance, pulling them off the shelves.

"Damn, girl, look at you in that bikini." She was gorgeous—slender, lean and tanned.

She scoffed, sipping her wine. "I was just a baby then."

"I bet you still rock a bikini, no problem." I flipped the page, finding more pictures of a girl on spring break, bright eyes and bare midriffs. "I wish I could say the same!"

"Are you kidding me? Mandy, you're gorgeous."

"Meh. I'm old." I rolled my eyes, flipping another page. "Tom better marry me soon or I'm gonna die old and alone with just my vibrator for company."

Jen laughed, stretching out on the bed beside me on her belly, mirroring my posture, kicking her feet up behind her. "Well, who needs them?"

"Men?" I smiled.

"Yeah." She turned her face to me, her eyes bright, curious. We were both more than a little drunk. "Tell me the truth—who do you have better orgasms with, Tom or your vibrator?"

"Well..." I pretended to consider this, but there was really only one answer.

She grinned. "Yeah, me too."

"What kind of vibrator do you have?" I pushed the photo album aside, turning toward her.

"Want to see it?" Her offer caught me off guard, making my heart race, but I wasn't about to turn her down.

"Yeah, sure."

She went to the place every girl keeps her vibrator—her underwear drawer—and pulled it out, looking both a little shy and a little proud. I had a few vibrators of my own, simple, streamlined things, but this was a monster, at least a foot long with a bright pink dick-head and what looked like—I swear to God—a rabbit attached to the base.

"Damn, girl—that's not a vibrator, that's a party in your pants!"

"It feels soooo good." Jen's eyes sparkled as she sat next to me on the bed, still holding the thing. Up close, I could see all the buttons and controls at the base, and yes, that was a little silicone rabbit attached. "Want to try it?"

"Are you serious?" I was just asking to be sure. My pussy was already soaking wet from being around her all night long.

Jen's shoulders sagged and she started to get up. "I'm sorry, I shouldn't have—"

"No, wait." My hand on her arm was electric, like we'd completed a circuit the moment I touched her. "I want to. I want to but..."

"But what?"

"I just wish we had two. So we could both... you know..." I flushed. There was no sense not going forward with it now. "Otherwise it might be awkward."

"I doubt that, but you're in luck." She smirked, handing me the pink vibrator and going back to her underwear drawer. She pulled out another vibrator, this one more familiar to me. Just a plain flesh-colored dildo with a simple dial control at the bottom. "This one isn't quite as fun as that one, but it'll do."

She took the initiative, unbuttoning her jeans and sliding them over her slim hips. She was gorgeous, every glorious inch of her. Her panties were gone in an instant, revealing the truth she'd stated earlier—Jen wasn't a real blonde at all. Her pussy was nicely trimmed, though—what else could you expect from a hairdresser?—a neat little landing strip on top and completely shaved down below.

I wanted to see her breasts too, but she was already climbing onto the bed, shoving the photo albums to the floor and stretching out beside me. I'd been too stunned by the sight of her to do anything with the vibrator in my hand, but when she spread her legs and turned hers on, I remembered my own.

"Ohhhh yes." Her eyes closed as she teased the fake cock head between her smooth lips, the buzz of it filling the room. "So good."

It was. My pussy throbbed and I squeezed my legs together, feeling the wetness in the crotch of my panties. Thankfully, I didn't have as much to take off to get to the goods. All I had to do was inch up my skirt and nudge my panties aside with the vibrator. Its pink head was soft silicone, not quite as good as a tongue but almost, and I rubbed it easily through my slick slit, watching Jen play with herself.

She opened her eyes briefly to glance at me, giving me a dreamy half-smile. "Don't forget to turn it on."

"Oh. Right." I was loathe to take the thing away from my pussy, but I had to inspect the controls. They were far too complicated for my booze-addled brain. "Are you sure this thing doesn't control the space shuttle?"

Jen giggled, half sitting to take it from me. It was still glistening with my juices and I watched, my heart caught in my throat, as she licked the head of it with the pointed, pink tip of her tongue.

"You're bad."

She gave a throaty laugh, flashing a mischievous smile before peeling off her t-shirt. "I can be far worse."

I would have been lying if I'd said I'd been hoping for anything different when she pushed my legs open wider and settled between them, now completely nude. Her breasts were small and ripe, like little plums, her nipples a dark contrast to her pale skin and the corn silk of her hair. I wanted to look at them more but she had settled on her belly, urging my hips up, pulling my panties off and showing me how to work the contraption in her hand.

"Like this." She pushed a button and the vibrator hummed to life between my legs. I tried to pay attention to her instructions—how to turn it up, how to change the pulse—but the way she had the head of it pressed right against my clit all the while made it far too difficult to concentrate on anything mechanical.

"Jen," I whispered, biting my lower lip. She was talking about the speeds—three of them I think? "Oh God... Jen..."

She lifted her blonde head, her eyes meeting mine, and smiled. "You like it on your clit?"

I moaned, shifting my hips forward and up in response. "Make it go faster."

"Okay." She did, and my thighs trembled, my pussy so wet I was sure I was soaking her bed. "Better?"

"Oh God, yes." The vibrations sent lovely shivers through me and I found myself unbuttoning my blouse and unhooking my bra without thinking, letting it fall open so I could tweak my nipples while she worked the head of the dildo over my sensitive clit.

"But you haven't really felt the full effect yet." Jen's remark would have opened my eyes, but it was the feel of the vibrator parting my swollen lips, sliding down to my hole, that really did it. I gulped and gasped but I let her slip it slowly in, the whole thing making my pelvis buzz.

"My clit," I protested. I was one of those girls who wanted—*needed*—direct clitoral stimulation.

"No worries, sweetheart." She pressed it in deeper and suddenly that pelvic hum became centered again right where I liked it. Gasping, I looked down to see the silicone rabbit pressing against my clit, the vibrator deep inside me now.

"Oh my god!" I reached out for something to hold onto, finding her wrist and forcing the toy even deeper, the rabbit's ears mashed against the aching bud of my clit, teasing me into submission. "That's fucking good!"

"Oh it gets better." Jen did something with the controls and before I knew what was happening, the whole thing was moving inside of me, turning in delicious circles.

"You weren't kidding!" I gasped. I didn't tell her that I normally didn't insert vibrators—I just used them to tease my clit to orgasm. But this! This thing was out of this world! It not only vibrated against my clit, but there were beads along the length that turned, little ridges teasing the walls of my pussy with every pass. I'd never felt anything like it.

"Told you." She smiled. "It makes me come so hard. It's fucking epic."

I could imagine. I was imagining. I wanted to find out! "Faster, Jen. Oh god, please."

"The vibration? Or the rotation? Or—"

"All of it!" I cried. I couldn't believe I was saying it, but I was. My whole pussy was spasming, aching for release. I couldn't hold it back. "Oh God, fuck me faster, harder, deeper!"

"Mmmm!" She did as I asked, so skilled with the thing I knew she must have fucked herself a thousand times with it. Thinking of her doing that—knowing this very vibrator had been inside of Jen's wet pussy—sent me flying into orbit.

"I'm gonna come!"

"Yes!" She shoved the vibrator in as far as it would go, giving me just what I wanted, and my body rocked hard on the bed, trembling and quivering with my climax. "Oh God. Oh my God that was so fucking hot. You made me so wet."

I wanted to see. I wanted to taste. But even though we were pretty well drunk and masturbating together on the bed, I still wasn't sure she wanted to go *that* far.

"You taste so fucking good." She slid the dildo out of me, licking the length, sucking the head into her mouth as she knelt up between my thighs. She was so beautiful she made me dizzy and watching her suck that cock was hot. Hotter than hot. My still-fluttering pussy ached in response.

"I bet you do, too."

"Want to find out?" she asked.

I nodded, too eager, but God, I did want to. So very much. I tingled all over at the thought of her hot, pink flesh under my tongue.

Jen stretched out on her back, spreading her long, slender thighs, and then her pussy, her perfectly manicured French nails slowly peeling back the layers like ripe fruit. My mouth was watering. She circled her clit with one finger, shivering, her nipples growing hard, as if there was a direct connection between the two.

I watched her touch herself, taking my blouse and bra off completely, and finally unzipping my skirt. When that was gone, I was left just as naked as she was. I settled myself between her thighs, just like she had between mine, but I wasn't armed with a dildo. All I had were my tongue and my fingers and I wondered if they would be adequate. She was rubbing herself furiously now, her breath coming fast, her cheeks rosy and flushed.

My pussy ached. She was so beautiful—I could have stayed there and watched her until the end of time. I knew I was hesitating. We'd already gotten naked and played with ourselves—and each other—but somehow this felt like crossing a line that couldn't be explained away in the morning as two horny drunk girls just having a little fun.

"Oh please," Jen begged, spreading her swollen pussy lips in front of me. "Your tongue. Please!"

It was her plea that decided me and finally did me in. I hadn't done it in a long, long time, but it came back to me in an instant. Not so much like riding a bike or driving a car. More like breathing after being underwater for a long time. She tasted like sweet heaven, pungent and strong, and I took my time getting to her clit, wanting to really take her in, exploring every slippery crack and crevice.

"Mandy!" she cried, impatient, her hands moving to my hair, guiding me. She wanted it, almost as much as I did, and I covered her with my mouth, warming her with my breath before focusing my tongue against the hard little nub of her clit. I felt her shudder, heard her breathe a sigh of relief—finally, finally, she was on the right path, headed in the direction of ecstasy.

Licking a girl's pussy for the very first time is always an experiment. Does she like it hard or soft? Fast or slow? Fingers or no? It's all trial and error. We women are far more complicated than the masculine rub and thrust release. I dialed my tongue around her clit, searching for the most sensitive spot. We all have one—mine is a little right of center, about two o'clock. Jen's was opposite mine. I could tell I hit the spot when she cried out, her hips jolting upward involuntarily toward my mouth.

Once I'd navigated to the perfect place, I stayed there, knowing how desperate she was, how much she wanted it. If she hadn't been so hot for it, I probably would have teased her more, nuzzling her thighs, licking at her labia. She was so baby-soft and smooth! But I didn't have the heart to make her wait. Besides, her hands were buried in my hair, hips rocking and rolling, heels dug deep into the bed.

"Ohhhhh fuck!" Her guttural cry made my tongue flutter faster, harder. I knew it couldn't be quite as intense as her vibrator, but I also knew how sweetly delicious a tongue was focused right at that magic spot. Nothing could quite match it or take its place. I slid my fingers through her slit, feeling how wet she was. If I'd been worried about soaking the bed, it didn't matter—Jen was even wetter than me, and I didn't think that was possible.

"Yes!" she gasped, thrusting toward my probing fingers. "Fuck me! Do it! Finger me hard while you lick my cunt!"

I squeezed my legs together, feeling the fiery throb of my own cunt, and thought I might just climax from her words. Dizzy with lust, unmindful of my newly-manicured fingernails, I slipped my fingers into her hole. She was smooth as silk, a velvet clutch and release.

"More!" she insisted, not shy now about telling me just what she wanted. She was too close to her goal for that. "Put them all in me! Stretch my pussy wide open!"

That wasn't so easy. She was tight, even though she was incredibly wet, but I managed to get three fingers in, giving them to her in fast, easy strokes. But that wasn't enough, not for Jen.

"Ohhhh God, don't stop!" she cried, fucking back against my hand, guiding my mouth onto her pussy, rubbing my whole face against it so I had to chase her clit with my tongue. "More! Oh fuck me more! Harder! Deeper! Faster!"

I groaned with the effort—my shoulder was actually aching—but I was so turned on I had to keep squeezing my legs together, afraid my pussy juices were going to run down my legs all over the bed like I'd wet myself. Besides, keeping it locked up tight that way felt so good. I knew I could come in an instant if I spread my legs and nudged my clit just a little bit, but I didn't want that. Not yet. I wanted to make her come first.

"Ohhhh fuck! Fuck! Fuck! Fuck!" She repeated it over and over as her belly began that telltale spasm, her pussy clutching at the deep thrust of my fingers. I fastened my mouth over her mound, sucking hard at her throbbing clit, her nails raking over my scalp as she bucked on the bed. Her orgasm left us both breathless and gasping for air, but when I lifted my head from between her legs, she grabbed a fist full of my hair and grinned.

"Don't stop," she whispered, spreading her swollen lips with the fingers of her other hand, showing me the damage I'd done. Her flesh had gone from pink to blush-red from my attention, her pussy juices pooling at her entrance, a creamy, sticky mess. "I want to come again."

My eyes brightened and I leaned in to capture her clit once more, feeling her whole body tremble, as if I'd given her an electric shock.

"Come here," she begged, reaching, grabbing for me. "Ohh God, Mandy, your tongue is so good!"

I swung my bottom around, letting her situate me, feeling her slender arms wrapped around my hips as she pulled my pussy down to her face.

Now it was my turn to swear. "Oh fuck!"

I knew I wasn't going to be able to stand that kind of attention for long. Her clit was thick and swollen against my tongue, and the way she moaned against my pussy when I licked it drove me wild. Jen was eager but skilled—she'd clearly done this before. She found my sensitive spot in moments, focusing there with a flutter and tickle that made my knees want to buckle.

Knowing now what she liked, I slid my fingers deep inside, hearing her groan in response, her hips rocking up to meet me. I fucked her hard and she fucked me right back, her muffled "mmm-mmm!" response hot against my flesh, which I could only translate as "more-more!"

But when she started to do the same, working a finger into my pussy, I wiggled in protest, unfastening my mouth long enough to explain.

"No fingers," I instructed. It was far too distracting. "Please, just my clit."

She focused her attention back on my clit, working magic with the flick of her tongue, sending heat through my whole body. My nipples were hard against her belly, and one of her hands found my breast, tweaking, squeezing, pushing me feverishly close to my destination. I knew I was going to come, but I wanted to make her come again too.

I worked my tongue and fingers together furiously, trying to stay centered on the task at hand, but her mouth was far too good, and the way she rolled my nipples while she licked me made it too hard to concentrate. That's when I saw the vibrator resting against her thigh.

It was the less-complicated one and I grabbed it, turning it on and replacing my fingers with its length. Jen cried out, losing her grasp on my pussy, as I began to fuck her with the dildo, using my tongue to tease her little clit. She seemed to like that, if the way she grabbed my hips and buried her face in my pussy was any indication. Her thighs were wide and trembling, her hips pushed up, the low, muffled sounds in her throat growing louder by the moment.

Then I pushed the speed even higher, feeling that first no-turning-back sensation in my groin, knowing my orgasm was coming and wanting her to get there too. Jen writhed beneath me, frenzied, her tongue and mouth going crazy against my pussy, and that sent me over the edge. I couldn't stop if it I tried. Delicious spasms wracked my whole body and I sucked Jen's clit between my lips to keep myself from screaming with pleasure.

And then she was coming too, in a flood of juices all over the plunging dildo in my hand, the wet sound of her orgasm filling the room. It went on and on, and I didn't stop fucking her or licking her for a moment, feeling her nails digging into my ass, leaving half-moon crescents I would notice later but I didn't notice at all then. Nothing in the world existed except the hot, sweet, pulsing pink flesh of Jen's pussy in my mouth.

"Holy fuck." She gasped against my thigh, leaving hot trails of kisses there. "I can't see straight."

"My ears are ringing," I panted, wiping her juices off my chin with the back of my hand as I rolled to the side, collapsing on the bed and staring up at the ceiling. It was spinning. Or maybe that was my head. I couldn't tell. "Now *that* was better than my vibrator."

"I'll say," she agreed, sighing happily. "How come guys can't learn to do that?"

I thought about Tom's brief forays between my legs, his eagerness to penetrate me, the unwillingness to learn my queues, even after years of being together.

Glancing over at Jen, I shrugged. "They probably could, if they wanted to."

We were quiet then, both of us, I think, contemplating that realization.

"I want to show you something." She went over to the television and turned it on. I couldn't believe she could stand, let alone walk, but I half-sat, back on my elbows, to watch as she put a disk into the DVD player. It was only a moment before she had queued it up to a lesbian scene, one of the women wearing a very large strap-on, the other bent over to take it.

"Hot," I murmured. It was. My pussy was still on fire but I couldn't help touching myself, exploring the wetness, the gentle pulse of my orgasm still fading. I couldn't believe it, but she made me want to come again. I didn't often have more than one climax in a session with Tom—honestly, I was lucky to get that. But Jen just made me want more. And more. And more.

"Isn't it?" She sat on the edge of the bed, glancing back at me with a little smile. "I let Brad watch lesbian porn and jerk off whenever he wants. He thinks he's buying it for himself."

I chuckled. "But you watch it when he's not home don't you?"

"Hell yes." She grinned, looking back at the screen with a longing sigh. "I want to do that."

"On top or bottom?"

"Bottom."

We were going to get along just fine, me and Jen. "Do you have a strap-on?"

"No." She sighed. "I've never had the opportunity to use one."

"Maybe you should get one." I sat up, steadying myself. I was still dizzy. Then I put my arms around her from behind, cupping her sweet breasts in my hands. They felt just like I knew they would, like firm little plums.

She moaned softly, leaning back against me, letting me fondle her. "I think maybe I should."

I had a feeling this was going to be the beginning of a beautiful, brand new sort of friendship.

Pajama Party

Armed and Ready.

That was the name of the nail polish Casey was using to paint my toenails. It was a ghastly color, a brownish army green with a pearlescent tint. But I consoled myself that it was better than the black licorice she'd painted her own toenails with. I was more into pretty pink polish with names like *Lovey Dovey* and *Jamaica Me Crazy*, but Casey's truth or dare question had hit far too close to home for my liking and I'd taken the dare instead. So I was letting her paint my toenails Baby-Shit-Brown—er, *Armed and Ready.* Anyway, it wasn't like nail polish remover hadn't been invented yet.

"So, truth or dare?" I slurped Peanut Butter Capt'n Crunch from my spoon, crunching happily. I'd won our cereal-eating contest—Casey had barely made it through her second bowl—and this was my prize. The entire box of Peanut Butter Capt'n Crunch was mine—all mine! I hadn't really eaten the stuff since we were thirteen or so, back when we used to do sleepovers like this on a weekly basis, but so far I wasn't disappointed with my re-acquaintance with it. Unlike the Spaghetti-O's we'd microwaved for dinner. I shuddered just thinking about it. We'd fed those to the dog.

Casey kept teasing me I was going to regret all this in the morning when I was puking up Capt'n Crunch along with all the wine we were drinking. Granted, the wine was definitely a new addition to our last sleepover of the summer—maybe our last sleepover ever. The thought made me sad and I gulped down the rest of my glass of wine, shuddering at the bitter taste it left in my mouth and following it quickly with another spoonful of cereal. Quite the combination!

"Truth." Casey leaned forward, holding her long blonde hair out of the way so she could blow on my toes to dry the polish. The sensation gave me chills.

I grinned at her response. We always said "truth" first. Of course, if the question was too difficult to answer, we switched to dare in an instant. It was technically against the rules, but we'd played that way forever.

"How big is Lance's dick?" I knew I'd surprised her with the question, but I couldn't help myself. I really, really wanted to know.

"April," she warned, putting the brush back into the bottle and twisting it closed, tossing it into the plethora of bottles jutting up haphazardly on the bedspread in a myriad of colors.

"Come on." I leaned forward, conspiratorial. "You used to tell me everything. So spill. Does Lance have a nice, big... *lance*?" I waggled my eyebrows at her for effect.

She cleared her throat and shrugged. "It's... sufficient."

"Sufficient?" I gaped at her, appalled. "You poor, poor girl!"

"Oh shut up." She grabbed the little plastic tub off my night table and started putting the nail polish bottles away. "Look who's talking. You haven't had a cock in over a year!"

"So let me live vicariously." I grinned. "And you know that's not a real answer. I want a measurement."

Casey sniffed, setting the full tub aside. "I've never measured."

"I bet *he* has. Every guy does." I wiggled my toes, testing the polish, making sure it was dry before hopping off the bed. "I have an idea."

"Where are you—?"

I ignored Casey's question, running to my mother's room. No one was home. My mom and stepdad had gone to her high school reunion thing three hours away and were staying there overnight. They trusted me, and why wouldn't they? I'd never given them any reason not to. They'd left us alone during sleepovers for years, and the only trouble we'd gotten into was eating too much pizza and watching movies until three in the morning. Besides, I knew they'd rather have us at our house alone than at Casey's house with her drunken stepfather. He was always home—always out of work—while Casey's mother worked two jobs, one cleaning floors during the day at Target, the other at night tending bar.

"April, what—?" Casey's eyes widened when I leapt back into the room and she saw what I was brandishing like a sword in my left hand.

"Remember this?" We'd first discovered it on a foray into my mother's bedroom looking for make-up, jewelry and dress-up clothes when were about thirteen.

She snorted laughter. "Who could forget *The Terminator*?"

"So, using this as a model..." I plopped onto the bed, tossing the monster dildo between us. It was at least a foot long—maybe more—big, black and formidable. "How big is Lance's cock?"

She picked up the toy, a little smirk on her face, and I just knew she was remembering the first time we'd found it, both of us giggling and horrified. What would you do with such a thing, we'd wondered? Neither of us would have an experience with actual male genitalia for years, and I have to admit, the first time I saw a real cock, I'd been a little disappointed.

The Terminator had given me very distorted expectations!

"I can't." She put it down, shaking her head. "Lance would kill me."

"He doesn't need to know." I picked the toy up, hefting it my hand. "Come on. Is it this big?" I slid my finger along the veined length, about five inches from the tip. "This big?" I waggled my eyebrows, going a little further, about eight inches now. "This big?"

I raised my eyebrows and smirked, holding the whole, humungous thing between my palms.

"Dare! I'll take the dare!" Casey countered, vehemently shaking her head at me and batting the toy away when I leaned in toward her with it.

"Okay, fine." I twisted the knob at the bottom of the dildo, making it hum to life. "I dare you to fuck yourself with *The Terminator*."

"April!" Her jaw dropped. She was truly shocked. "You're crazy!"

"So tell me then, how big is Lance's dick?" I had her cornered and we both knew it.

She was going to have to tell me, and once she opened those floodgates, I was hoping for a deluge of information. We'd always talked about our boyfriends and every little thing that happened on our dates, from first kisses to rounding first base to first times. We shared everything. Until Lance. What was it about this guy that made Casey clam up?

"You're a brat, April Cohen!" she hissed at me.

"It's truth or dare, remember?" I raised my eyebrows at her, wielding *The Terminator* menacingly. "I *double*-dog dare you! If you're not going to tell me the truth, you *have* to take the dare."

"I do not." She stood and walked away, taking the tub of nail polish, her back to me as she put it on my dresser, but I could see her face in the mirror. I didn't like that look—sad and a little... scared? Of what?

I frowned and bit my lip, considering, looking at my best friend in her UCLA sweats and t-shirt. This time next week, she would be soaking up the California sunshine, and I'd be walking on the campus of Boston U amidst the changing autumn colors. It would be the first time since fourth grade music camp we'd be separated for a significant length of time.

"Well you know what this means." I stood, coming up behind her, meeting her eyes in the mirror. I looked ready to go to prom, aside from the baby-doll nightie, my hair all up and curled, make-up perfect.

"No..." Casey's voice trailed off, her eyes widening slowly with dawning realization as a mischievous smile spread across my face. "Nooo!"

But it was too late.

"Tickle penalty!" I grabbed for her as she ran, catching the waistband of her sweats as she dove toward my bed.

Casey howled, twisting and laughing already, even though I hadn't touched her yet. Her sweats slipped further down her hips as she made another attempt to get further away, already begging me, *"Please no no no, don't, not the tickle penalty, not the tickle penalty!"*

I leaned against her legs on the bed, pinning her, getting ready for my tickle assault, when I glanced down and saw the bruises. These weren't just a few "Oops I ran into the coffee table" sort of bruises either. These spread across her behind like a Canadian sunrise, all oranges and blues and purples.

I couldn't help the gasp that escaped my throat.

Casey looked back at me, wide-eyed, horrified. "Get off me!"

"What happened?" I whispered. I couldn't take my eyes off the damage. Then I saw a tell-tale bruise on her hip as she turned, her sweats pulling down further as she tried to get away—a large handprint, definitely four fingerprints, like grip marks. A man's hand. "Oh my god, it was Lance, wasn't it?"

I felt Casey's whole body collapse beneath me, boneless, face buried in her arms. I climbed to the side, stretching out beside her on the bed, speechless. And furious. I'd been resentful of Lance and the Casey-time he'd stolen from me all summer, but while my friend had grown more and more distant, I'd never suspected anything like *this*.

"I'm going to kill that bastard," I said through clenched teeth, reaching out to stroke her fine, blonde hair.

"April," Casey warned, turning her tear-streaked face to look at me.

"Don't 'April' me!" I scoffed. "He deserves to be drawn and quartered!"

"I know." Her voice was barely a whisper, her eyes welling up with tears.

I leaned in close and pressed my forehead to hers like we used to, hiding under the covers with a flashlight to read Goosebumps books late into the night, making our blanket-tent warm with our breath.

"That black eye you got last month wasn't from softball, was it?" I tucked a bit of blonde fluff behind her ear. There was still a ghost of it around her eye socket.

She shook her head, miserable. "He stopped leaving marks where people could see…"

I blinked, feeling my hand clenching into a fist at the thought of him hurting her. "You can't see him anymore."

"I'm not." She sniffed, wiping at an errant tear. "This was… the last. Even his mother says he has 'anger management issues.' Besides, I'm going away to school."

"This is an 'anger management' issue like Charlie Sheen has a drug problem!" I should have known. Casey had only been with two other boys, and only one of them had done anything sexual with her. Lance was her first real relationship. I was kicking myself for not seeing the signs. "Did you tell him you're breaking up with him?"

"I was afraid," she whispered, her eyes spilling over with tears. "I'm afraid."

I put my arms around her, felt her trembling, and tried to keep the rage in my chest from bursting out and chasing Lance Dawson down like an animal. I tried not to dwell on what I wanted to do to him—and how protracted and satisfying such torture might be. I couldn't believe I'd been jealous, that all this time I'd been dwelling on how *I* felt, missing out on time with my best friend, when I should have been paying attention to *her,* noticing the signs—the freaking *obvious* signs!

"I'm so sorry." I shook my head against hers, closing my eyes and feeling them sting with my own tears.

"It's not your fault."

"He picked you instead of me," I reminded her—reminded us both.

"I know." She winced. "I was so damned proud of that."

I remembered. She'd been so excited when he'd asked her out, when he chose *her*. Casey was dainty and really quite pretty, but she wasn't overtly so. She was a sort of behind-her-glasses pretty, under her baggy sweats and sweatshirts.

But that day she'd borrowed one of my bikinis and her glasses had been tucked into her beach bag, and Lance, a tall, tanned lifeguard with aviator sunglasses that hid his eyes, had seemed particularly focused on her shyness, the way she cast her gaze down and smiled at the sand, her cheeks pinking up when he talked to her.

Now I knew why.

"He picked you for a reason." The words burned my throat. I didn't want to hurt her—but she had to know.

"Because I'm stupid." Her lower lip trembled and I touched it with my index finger.

"Because you're vulnerable."

She snorted. "Desperate."

"Eager." I rubbed her lower lip thoughtfully with my thumb, remembering how bruised and swollen it had been earlier this summer, how she'd claimed she'd run into the side of the bathroom door in the middle of the night.

"Needy."

I smiled. "Naïve."

"Stupid." She sniffed. "But I thought... I really thought... he was the only one who would ever want me."

"Now *that's* stupid." I did it without thinking. Or maybe I'd been thinking it all along. I leaned in and kissed her, her lips soft and slightly salty from her tears. She tasted like Spaghetti-Os and wine. She was delicious.

"What are you doing?" Casey breathed as we parted.

"Showing you." I lifted her t-shirt, heady from the wine and intent on proving her wrong. I had to fix this thing somehow. I should have protected her. I should have been there. How could I not have seen what was happening? She was beautiful, she was perfect—and Lance was definitely not the only person who would ever want her.

I wanted her.

I'd always wanted her.

"April…" Her whisper was a warning, but I didn't heed it. Instead, I trailed kisses up her quivering belly, finding her braless, and it was no wonder. Her breasts were bruised too, dirty fingerprints all over her, like tattoos. This is what she hadn't wanted me to see, why she'd refused to dress up tonight during our make-over session.

"Poor baby." I kissed her bruises, every one, while she watched, her face pained. "Am I hurting you?"

She shook her head, tracing one of the bruises near her pale pink nipple with a black-painted nail. "He likes it rough."

"I'd like to give it to *him* rough," I snarled, nuzzling her hand out of the way and kissing that bruise too. "How do *you* like it, Casey?"

"I don't know," she whispered. At that moment, I couldn't help remembering how we'd practiced kissing our pillows when we were young, how she had puckered like a fish and we'd giggled ourselves silly.

I felt a slow grin starting to spread. "Want to find out?"

Her lips parted slightly and she wet them with the tip of her tongue before asking, "With you?"

I nodded.

"Yes, please."

Her assent gave me the courage to kiss her again, deeper this time, my tongue finding hers, the sharp intake of her breath allowing further exploration. I blamed the wine. I blamed Lance and his 'anger management issues.' I blamed the fact that I'd been celibate myself for over a year.

But the truth was I wanted her. I wanted her so much I couldn't breathe, couldn't think. If I was thinking anything, I was thinking how much I was going to miss her, how much I loved her, how long I'd wanted to do this very thing as my hand moved up to cup her breast and thumb her nipple, feeling her knees opening under mine in sweet acquiescence.

Her sweats were already half-off, her panties edging down with them, and I tugged them down her thighs as we kissed, kneeing and toeing them off her silky smooth legs. We undressed in front of each other all the time, but this was different. We both knew what was happening here, could feel it building with the rise of our breath, the increased pounding of our hearts. I felt her hesitation in the way she turned her head to catch a breath, eyes fluttering open momentarily to shyly meet mine, her mind fighting with the overwhelming sensation, and I didn't want her head to win out.

Thank god we'd both already consumed a bottle and a half of wine.

I moved lower to lap softly at her nipple, letting her close her eyes again and lose herself in the sensation, feeling the pink nub puckering between my lips. My hand found its way between her legs and I moaned against her breast when I found her, baby-smooth and soft, her pussy lips slightly parted. So wet already! She was beautiful, in spite of the bruising, like a sweet peach, overripe and ready.

"You're shaved," I murmured in surprise, realizing I hadn't seen her naked since early summer, when we changed into our suits at the pool. That was where she'd met Lance.

Casey grimaced, her eyelids fluttering open. "He made me."

"I like it."

That was a lie. I *loved* it. The soft skin of her labia under my fingers made me drunk with lust, my mouth watering to taste her. While I'd told Casey about *most* of my firsts—with boys—I'd never told her about the other times, the summer camp fumblings with the other girls, soft kisses in the dark at sleepovers like this one that led to so very much more.

- 51 -

But somehow it was always Casey I was thinking about, even then.

"Did he ever lick you?" I inquired, swallowing my distaste at the thought of Lance anywhere near this plump, luscious little mound of flesh.

"Some." She made a face, squirming on the bed and looking down at me now with wide-open eyes. She looked uncomfortable, a little scared, like she might change her mind at any minute, and I didn't want that to happen.

"Let's see if you like this." I covered her with my mouth, unable to help the soft caught cry in my throat as I explored the smooth texture of her skin, delving deeper to taste her more fully. Her clit was easy to find, hooded and fat at the top of her cleft. I wanted to take time to drink her in, trace the labyrinth of her soft, pink folds, but I wanted her to forget her reluctance more.

Casey gasped as I began to flick her clit with my tongue, the expert movements more than enough to send her headlong down Forgetful Lane. She breathed my name, hands fisting the covers as sensation took over, toes curling and uncurling against the mattress as I worked my mouth against her pussy, knowing just how good what I was doing felt for her. There was nothing like a hot, wet tongue bathing your clit. It was sensation beyond sensation and my own pussy clenched in response and anticipation.

"Good?" I took a moment to take a breath and ask, although from the half-lidded look on her face, the way her lips were parted, her breath coming fast, I didn't really have to.

"Fucking great," she moaned, shifting her hips toward me, giving me better access. Then she opened her eyes and frowned, cocking her head at me. "Are you stopping?"

I snorted a laugh. "Are you kidding me?"

She flushed prettily, not just her cheeks but her neck and chest too. "Lance stopped. He'd do it for a minute or two, but then… it was like he got bored."

And I thought I wanted to kill him before? Just looking at the fingerprints on her thighs where he'd grabbed her made me want to throttle him, but knowing in the end he'd done nothing but use her for his own pleasure without any thought or care for her at all made me blind with anger.

"You taste so fucking good, I could eat you all night long." I feathered kisses over her clit, teasing, making her bite her lip and spread even wider for me.

"Ohhh God." Her head went back when I gently sucked her clit between my lips, holding it there so I could tease it with my tongue, back and forth, back and forth. Her pussy was so wet there was a little circle of juices darkening my bedspread beneath her, and I could already imagine myself touching that spot when she was gone—touching it, licking it, rubbing myself against it. I wanted all of her, every bit. I didn't want to spill a single drop.

Casey's hips began to move in rhythm, her breath coming even faster now, her cheeks flushed with rosy color. Both of her nipples were pursed and hard, and I could see gooseflesh spreading across her trembling inner thighs and lower belly. Her whole body was alive, thrumming with her impending orgasm—and I was going to take her there.

"Please," she begged, tossing her head wildly from side to side. "Oh God, please! Don't stop! Don't!"

"Nnn-nnnnn," I managed, shaking my head, sucking and licking furiously at her clit as I pressed my fingers against her sex, right up against her opening. I didn't put them in, but I kept them pressed flat there, providing a steady pressure and heat, feeling the first beginning flutters of her climax. She was close.

"Oh! April! Oh my God!"

Very close.

I slid my other hand up the taut stretch of her belly to her breast, squeezing and rolling her nipple between my thumb and forefinger, as if I could fine-tune her orgasm. And maybe I could, after all.

Casey gasped and bucked her hips up, giving me the hot, pink flesh of her pussy completely, drowning me in her juices. I groaned, swallowing and swallowing, feeling the muscles between her pussy and her ass contracting against my palm as I moved to cup her sex with my whole hand, parting my fingers to leave room only for my mouth.

"Ooooohhhhh!" Her body shook and jerked, as if she was being hit with huge volts of electricity, and I slowly eased away from her clit with my mouth, covering her now completely with my hand, feeling the hot, gentle throb of her sex. Her breathing was still fast, her face pink, her hair a golden cloud. When she slowly opened her eyes to meet mine, I saw the beginnings of a bemused smile playing on her lips.

"So… do you like that?" I rested my cheek against her thigh, feeling the muscles there still taut.

"Mmmm." She nodded happily. "*Uber*-like."

I giggled, rocking my palm against her. "Would you like it again?"

"Again?" she squeaked. "Now?"

"I bet you could." I grinned, sliding my hand down, parting her soft, sticky pussy lips with two fingers. "The second one is even better than the first, you know."

"It is?" Her eyes lit up in anticipation. "Ohhhh, God, but it's too sensitive!"

"That goes away." I kissed away her protest, the lightest press of my lips over her labia, not coming her near her clit, not yet. Now I could take my time, exploring the convoluted pink flesh between her legs, an exquisite labyrinth I could get lost in all night long, if she'd let me. The thought that she just might let me, given how she was responding now with soft sighs and shifting hips, made the ache in my own pussy almost unbearable. Almost.

"But… April…" I felt her hand moving in my hair, brushing it out of my face. "What about you?"

I shook my head in spite of the way my pelvis rocked against the bed at her words. "No, sweetie, this is about you, not me."

My God, she tasted good. The wet, dark circle beneath her had doubled in size and I was now determined to triple it—quadruple it. To infinity and beyond!

"April, I want to." Casey half sat, leaning back on her elbows to peer down at me between her thighs. "Please?"

I breathed in the scent of her, giving her pussy another long, soft kiss before I slid my body up to meet hers in response.

"Taste." And I kissed her, forcing my tongue between her lips, giving her that sweet, musky tang on my tongue. She was quite still at first, letting me share it with her, and I guessed it must have been the first time she had tasted her own pussy. I licked softly at her lower lip as we parted, looking into her eyes. "Well?"

"You're right." She smiled slowly. "I taste great."

I grinned back. "Fucking-A you do."

"Now let me taste you," she insisted, taking my breath away when she leaned in for more, kissing me, not soft and sweet, but hard and wanting, her arms going around my neck, her tongue probing, oh God, *sucking* on mine. I let her do it. We rolled back and forth on the bed until Casey was on top of me, her pussy positioned just over mine, the heat of her incredible.

"Are you sure?" I watched, breathless, as she pushed up my baby doll nightie and nuzzled my hard nipples through my bra. I undid it for her with a smile, watching her eyes light up—oh she was so fucking sweet—before beginning to lick and suck at them.

"Oh yes, definitely." Her tongue bathed me like a kitten's, over and over, every sensation like a jolt down between my thighs. "It feels so good. You have to know."

I do, I thought, but I didn't tell her that. Besides, I was ready to come just *thinking* about her face between my legs.

"Then let's do it together."

She cocked her head, frowning. "How?"

"I'll show you." I grabbed her, swinging her hips, positioning her so that I could wrap my arms around her hips and pull her pussy down to my mouth.

"Oooooo!" she squealed, giggling. "That's brilliant."

Fucking brilliant indeed. Now that I had her pussy, I didn't care what she did or didn't do to mine. Even if she just *breathed* on me, that would be more than enough.

But that isn't all she did.

While I spread her pussy lips and really looked at her, all pink and open and wet, Casey yanked my panties off and did the same. I could almost feel the heat of her gaze on me, looking at the dark, wiry triangle of hair I had left above my cleft, pointing at my shaved-bare slit. When I slid a finger between her slick lips, she did the same to me, nice and slow, playing in the juices. When I kissed her thighs, nuzzling her at the bend, she did too, sending shivers through me. When I touched my finger to her clit, nudging it back and forth, my clit finally got some attention too, making me moan softly and rock my hips.

So this was our game.

Monkey see, monkey do.

I slowly started kissing the glossy, swollen mound of flesh of her pussy, feeling her breath on mine, tentative, feathery kisses. Her lips were fat, thick and pink with the heat of her pulse, her clit protruding at the top of her crevice. I touched my tongue to it—I couldn't help it, I wanted her mouth on mine so much I could barely stand it—flicking the fleshy hood up and down, as if it was a tiny little cock with an itty-bitty foreskin.

"Oh, April." She squirmed on top of me, spreading her thighs wider. "That's nice."

"Mmmm." I agreed, teasing her clit, the feel of her breath almost enough to send me over. Then her tongue found me, a slow, tentative lick, like she was tasting a new flavor of ice cream. I moaned and shuddered, swallowing the taste of her.

"Oh wow." Her breath heated my pussy, her fingernails trailing lightly over my thighs. "That's…"

"You don't have to," I reminded her, breathless.

But her next words made me quake from the inside out. "Yummy!"

Oh yes. *Yes, yes, yes.*

Her clit throbbed under my tongue. God, I wanted to make her come in my mouth again. I wanted to make her come and come until she screamed so loud the neighbors called to see if someone was being murdered next door. But I held still, just trying to concentrate on breathing, trying not to be distracted by the taste of her on my tongue, the way her ass rose up in the air, her pussy juices running down my chin, waiting to see what she would do.

"Like this?" Her tongue, lapping, back and forth, oh heaven, *just like that, angel, just like that.*

"Perfect," I whispered, taking her clit between my lips and sucking gently.

"Oh!" She shifted her hips, bringing her belly down lower for me. "That's distracting."

"Can you reach *The Terminator*?" I asked, trying to see around her thighs. It was still humming gently, buried somewhere in the covers.

"Uh-huh." Casey found it, the sound growing louder as she uncovered it. "Got it. Oh no… you're not going to use this on me, are you?"

"No." I smiled, opening my thighs a little wider and lifting my hips. "You're going to use it on me."

"Ohhhh."

"Put it in." I was trying hard not to beg.

"It's so big!"

I groaned. "I know. Please."

Then she did it, easing the head of the dildo between my swollen lips. I was so wet, it slid in easily, and I heard her gasp.

- 57 -

"Fuck me, Casey," I urged, nuzzling at her pussy, her clit, rubbing her juices all over my face. I wanted to cover myself with her. "In and out... ohhhh God, yes. Like that."

"Can I lick you too?" she asked, but she already was, her tongue moving over my clit, the dildo plunging in and out, a nice, fast rhythm that was guaranteed to make me explode in under two minutes.

"Oh yes!" Oh God, the feel of her mouth, her hair brushing my thighs, the thrust of the cock between them—was this really happening?

"Faster?"

I groaned and thrust up. "Harder!"

"Doing this makes my pussy so wet," she breathed, wiggling on top of me.

"You taste so fucking good." I buried my face between her legs, wrapping my arms around her ass to bring her in close and tight. My tongue found her clit and focused, back and forth, right on her clit, a motion I could maintain no matter what, thank God, because my own pussy was on fire, the sensation rocking my whole body.

"Will you make me come again?" she begged. "Please?"

"Yes!" I gasped. "Just... just please don't stop."

"No." I heard her smile, but then there weren't any more words, just the sound of the vibrator plunging into my wetness and our soft moans of pleasure as we took each other to the edge of bliss. I couldn't tell where I ended and she began, our breath heating up the whole room, making it humid and wet, like our bodies.

And then I felt her stiffen and knew she was going to come again for me. I didn't hesitate, my tongue flickering lightning fast against her clit, eagerly lapping at her over and over, determined to take her there. Casey cried out and shuddered on top of me, but she never stopped fucking me—or licking me. She sucked my clit between her lips as she came, every spasm of her pussy mirrored by the suckle of her little mouth.

"Oh fuck!" I cried as her climax began to fade, her hips slowing. "I'm gonna come!"

She moaned and sucked faster, thrusting the dildo in deep and hard, keeping it there, and that was it—I was exploding, the earth falling away, every bit of me shattered into a zillion pieces, floating like stardust into nothing. And then it was Casey calling me back, my ears ringing, feeling her crawling up next to me to pull the covers over us both.

"Thank you." My best friend looked at me with tears in her eyes and my belly clenched. I touched her cheek, trailing a fingernail down her neck, over her exposed breast, where the bruises stood out like ink on her flesh. I was thinking about the most gratifying, horrible ways to torture Lance, but I knew what I would do instead. In the morning, Casey and I would tell my stepfather about what he'd done. My stepfather was a cop. He would know how to handle it best.

"So now you know what Casey likes," I whispered, kissing the tip of her nose and pulling her close to me.

"What Casey *loves.*"

I smiled, drifting, dreamy. The words just slipped out. "I love you, too."

The ensuing silence was like a knife in my heart.

And then she said, "I know."

I lifted my head to look at her, and I saw it clearly in her eyes. Had she known all along? Did it matter?

When I kissed her, putting everything I felt into it, she kissed me back, and I knew it didn't matter if we were going to be at two different schools on separate coasts. We were going to be best friends—the very best of everything, together—forever.

Moms' Night Out

"You look like you're trying to fit two bowling balls into a slingshot." Caroline watched in the bathroom mirror as Jaime, bent over, attempted to wiggle her milk-filled breasts into a pink bra at least two sizes too small.

"They're impossible!" Jaime sighed, lifting her breasts to show her considerable cleavage.

Caroline set down her mascara in the hot mess of make-up, hair product and baby wipes on the crowded sink before heading to the bedroom across the hall. She returned in a flash, holding two of Jaime's sports bras, one white and one black. Jaime was still wiggling away.

"Here, try one of these—a nursing mother's best friend on a night out. And hurry, I know you just pumped for the sitter, but I can practically see you filling from here." Caroline handed Jaime the sports bras and moved around behind her to help her unhook. "These should help keep things compressed enough all night."

Jaime straightened, stretching her arms up to let Caroline undo her and slip off the too-small bra, her wet eyes on the verge of tears.

Poor thing, Caroline thought, seeing the younger woman's emotions ready to spill out just like her engorged breasts in the tight fabric of her too-small bra. Jaime gasped as Caroline slipped the sports bra gently over her full breasts, her nipples hardening immediately.

"Sorry, I know how you feel, but you're just, well—so big! Dunno if I could handle twins!"

"What choice do I have?" Jaime crossed her arms under her heavy breasts and palmed her sensitive nipples to rub them. Still watching in the mirror, Caroline's brows rose and eyes widened as she caught Jaime, eyes closed, in a sigh that was both pain and pleasure at the same time. She knew the feeling well enough herself. "You know, when Rob was last home on leave, I couldn't keep him off them. He even wanted to, you know, fuck them until I was *so* sore. It was like having three babies, I swear! I felt like the Dairy

- 60 -

Queen!" Jaime's eyes fluttered open and she gave a shy smile and blush as she realized Caroline was admiring her.

The young women held each other's gaze in the mirror for a beat before Jaime broke the moment with a glowing pulse of the blush in her cheeks and neck and an embarrassed outburst. "Well, you know it's true, Caroline! You know it is! No one talks about it but we all know it...if it didn't feel good we wouldn't do it, right? Oh, Caroline I don't know if I can even do this anymore. Tell me I'm doing the right thing. Please? Rob hasn't been the same since his first tour in Iraq, and this separation, or divorce—oh, who the hell knows with him—is killing me!" The tears finally came.

Caroline wrapped her arms around Jaime from behind and Jaime gripped her hands and pulled her closer.

"Oh, hon, you know you're crazy with the hormones, and we both know you'll do whatever's best for those two babies. We always do. I think it was easier for me, knowing The Asshole—don't laugh, that's an official title—knowing I'd never see him again after he saw Kyle's heart beating on that ultrasound DVD I slipped in on him instead of last night's band video. Rock-A-Billy Zombies...who the hell leaves their baby momma for something called the Rock-A-Billy Zombies? Well, my little man and me, we don't need the chicken-shit anyway!"

"I don't know how to do this without Rob." Jaime's lower lip trembled and Caroline had an incredible urge to kiss it and make it all better. *Poor thing*, she thought again. Instead, she touched her finger to her friend's bottom lip as if to silence her.

"We'll do it together, how about that?"

"Thanks." Jaime put her head on Caroline's shoulder. "I don't know what I would have done if we hadn't met."

Caroline gave her a gentle squeeze. "Well, we can thank the Mommy and Me group for that tonight—if we make it. Come on, let's get you cleaned up, or we're going to miss the appetizers. And if you can't have drinks, at least you can pig out on those, since you're burning an extra thousand calories a day!"

"Okay." Jaime brightened, turning toward the mirror and adjusting her sports bra over the mounds of her breasts before reaching for the glittery black top hanging on a hook behind the bathroom door. "Let's get this party started!"

"That's my girl." Caroline grinned, nodding in approval as Jaime slipped her top on. Both women startled when Jaime's apartment intercom buzzer sounded. "And there's our babysitter!"

Jaime dabbed at her wet eyes with Kleenex. "Can you get it?"

"Sure."

The thirty-free-days of supersitters.com had paid off. Jeanie was not much older than the two young mothers, maybe late twenties, but she was all Nanny and the Professor...calm, warm and organized—minus the British accent.

The babies were asleep in what passed for the nursery of Jaime's two-bedroom apartment, with Caroline's little man, eighteen-month-old Kyle, asleep in the Pack 'n Play— hopefully for the night. The twins, of course, would be up to eat again and Jeanie called off her checklist, double checking the supply of Jaime's pumped milk in the fridge, as Caroline and Jaime finished getting ready for Moms' Night Out—the first one they'd been able to afford since joining the Mommy and Me group, and then only because they had pooled their money for a sitter.

As the two young mothers said good-bye-thank-yous and ran out the door ten minutes late, they turned around for each other to check hair, face, butt, legs and shoes, but they forgot to double check for the portable breast pump Caroline had brought in her purse. Jaime's breast pump was a Craig's List model, in great shape, and okay for lunchtime at the elementary school where she taught, but far too big for a Moms' Night Out at Olive Garden. There it sat on Jaime's bed in a pile of unchosen skirts and stockings as the door clacked closed.

Neither of them realized it until their entrees arrived, the restaurant packed, their table of ten women chattering and laughing louder than most. Caroline was on her third margarita—since Jaime couldn't drink and served as the perfect designated driver—and she was feeling it, her face flushed, her skin tingling. That's when Jaime leaned over and whispered, "I'm leaking," and Caroline checked her purse for the pump, shaking her head, wide-eyed with dismay, when she came up empty-handed, and both women sat, open-mouthed, blinking at each other in disbelief.

"Everything okay?" Nicki asked, eyes slanting as she watched Jaime slip out of her chair. Nicki was the head of their Mommy and Me group and ran it like a cross between a military operation and American Idol. There was an interview process to get in, and once accepted, you had to commit to two functions per month, or you were tossed out.

"Just a bathroom break." Caroline watched her friend threading her way through the tables. It was her fault Jaime was in this mess and she felt awful. Not only that, but if they had to go home early, both of them might get tossed out of the group. *Did half a night count?* she wondered.

Caroline stood, dropping her napkin onto her chair. "Be right back."

She found Jaime in the bathroom, as she'd expected, locked into one of the stalls. Caroline knocked. Olive Garden had completely private stalls, which she remembered well from nursing Kyle. She used to be too shy to breastfeed in public and would only come to the Olive Garden for dinner whenever the opportunity arose because they had such ample bathroom privacy. Of course, it wasn't easy balancing on a toilet to feed a baby, but beggars couldn't be choosers. Caroline smiled at the memory of her anxiety about public nursing. By the time Kyle was eight months and old enough to lift her shirt, she would whip it out anywhere.

"Sweetie? It's me. Open up."

The lock slid over and the door swung open, revealing a dejected Jaime sitting fully clothed on the toilet, stuffing folded paper towels into her bra. Caroline's heart melted. If only she hadn't forgotten the damned pump!

"I'm leaking like crazy. It's killing me! They're so tender!" Jaime wailed, pulling a wad of paper towel out. It was literally dripping with milk. "What am I going to do? I don't want to have to go home."

"I know, hon, me neither." Caroline cocked her head, frowning as she watched Jaime reach for toilet paper, wadding it up in her hand. Caroline stopped her. "Wait."

Jaime looked up, quizzical. "You got a better idea?"

"I actually do." Caroline took her friend's hands, pulling her to her feet. Their eyes locked and Caroline felt a flutter of excitement and anxiety in her belly. "Do you trust me?"

"Yeahhhh…" Jaime's face told a different story, but she allowed Caroline to move around her, the women trading places, Caroline sitting and Jaime standing.

"Okay, close your eyes," Caroline instructed.

"What?"

"Trust me." She was drunk, she knew it—and maybe, she decided, she could use that as an excuse later. She'd done a lot of things that seemed like a good idea at the time when she was drunk, things she had simply wanted to do but hadn't the courage. This, she decided, was one of those situations where she might say she was remorseful later and blame it on the margaritas—but in her heart, she knew she wouldn't really regret it for a minute.

"Okay." Jaime sighed, closing her eyes and shaking her blonde head as Caroline began to lift her friend's shirt up over her belly. "What are you—?"

"Shh!" Caroline chided, pulling Jaime's shirt off and gently freeing her heavy breasts from her sports bra. "Keep them closed."

Jaime was nude from the waist up now, wearing just a black mini and heels, and she was shivering. Her nipples were hard and beads of milky-white fluid gathered at the tips, falling in fat droplets to the bathroom floor. Caroline took in the breathless sight of her briefly before cupping one of her friend's breasts in her hands and beginning to suckle.

"Caroline! No! Oh my god! No! What...?"

Caroline didn't let up, suckling hard, swallowing deeply. She hadn't given any thought to how breast milk and margaritas were going to mix, but Jaime's milk was sweet and went down like cream. Jaime's hands went to Caroline's hair, at first attempting to push her off, her thin, lithe body squirming against the side of the bathroom stall as if she could wiggle away.

"Nooo!" Jaime wailed, but Caroline watched her friend's face, seeing the immediate relief there. "Oh... oh... that's... that's so much better already!"

"You said Rob did this, right?" She took a brief moment to ask the question before beginning to suckle again. There was so much milk it flooded her mouth instantly and Caroline swallowed and swallowed, looking up at Jaime as she opened her eyes in wonder, watching her friend's mouth work against her breast.

"Yeah, he likes it." Jaime flushed. "I always said he was stealing the baby's milk to make him stop, but he knew better."

"It's true." Caroline grinned up at her, lips wet with milk. "It's like the Doritos slogan—eat all you want, we'll make more."

"It's true. Plus it *does* feel good." Jaime giggled and bit her lip, looking shyly down at her friend. "Oh God, please, will you do the other one too?"

Caroline's only answer was to cup Jaime's other breast in both hands, stretching to cover her pink nipple with her mouth and beginning to suck. Jaime gave a little sigh, shifting her weight closer, giving Caroline more access. Jaime's milk came warm and fast and Caroline felt herself getting dizzy as she suckled and swallowed, hearing Jaime's breath coming faster, almost as fast as her own, soft mewls escaping her friend's throat.

"Is this turning you on as much as it is me?" She managed to gasp before leaning in to lick a rivulet of milk dripping down Jaime's firm breast, following the trail back up to her nipple so she could begin sucking again.

"Uh-huh," Jaime admitted, her eyes just slits, lips wet and parted, face and chest flushed.

"You can touch yourself," Caroline encouraged. She could feel how wet she was herself just from sucking on Jaime's nipples. She could barely keep her own hand from between her thighs. "Go ahead."

"Really?" Jaime whispered, glancing around, as if someone might see them, but the stall was enclosed, the bathroom empty. Caroline's tongue, making circles around her nipple now, no longer just serving the purpose of emptying her breasts of milk, relieving the pressure, but intentionally moving to give her pleasure, seemed to push Jaime over the edge. She hiked her skirt up, pushing the black panties she'd worn aside, giving Caroline a clear view of her curly blonde bush. She was so wet, her pubic hair was glistening in the fluorescents.

"Oh God…" Jaime gasped, sliding a finger between her fat pussy lips, easily circling her clit. Her voice was barely above a whisper. "Please… Please don't stop sucking…"

"I promise," Caroline breathed, her head moving back and forth, sucking first one, then the other. Jaime's fingers made a thick, squishy sound as she started to finger herself, eyes half-closed, breath coming even faster. "Oh you taste so good. Rub yourself off, hon, that's it. Faster. God that makes me so wet!"

Jaime opened her eyes and looked at her, cocking her head to the side. "Do you want to… you know…?"

"You don't care?" Caroline breathed, her pussy pulsing at the thought.

"No." Jaime blushed, but her fingers moved even faster. "I think it would be hot."

"Me too." Caroline moaned softly as she hiked up her own skirt, the crotch of her underwear almost as wet as Jaime's bra had been when she peeled it off. Her clit practically sighed in relief as she slid her hand under the elastic band of her panties and began to rub it. She couldn't help the moan that escaped her throat, but she kept her promise, her mouth fastened over Jaime's slick, milky nipple, sucking and swallowing at intervals.

"Oh yes, oh God, please..." Jaime gasped, her hand moving faster between her legs, her breathless begging giving Caroline goose bumps, her own hand rubbing furiously. Her pussy was on fire. The only sound aside from their hot, rapid breath was the wet plunge of Jaime's fingers and the gentle suck and swallow as Caroline took more of her friend's milk.

"Oh hon!" Caroline gasped, gulping another swallow of milk, unable to hold off any longer. "I'm going to make myself come!"

"Yes!" Jaime breathed, moaning and arching, offering her breasts. "Suck them! Suck my tits and make me come!"

Caroline gasped and buried her face against Jaime's breast, softer now, less engorged, but the nipples still hard and slick with milk. She sucked hard and deep, the cream thick and hot over her tongue as her orgasm crashed through her body, shuddering her against Jaime's slight frame.

"Oh! Oh! Coming! Ohhh!" Jaime quivered and spread her thighs wider, thrusting her hips forward as she came, and Caroline moaned in happy surprise when her mouth spontaneously began filling with milk. Jaime's other exposed breast did the same thing, shooting streams of milk, jets of it, over Caroline's shoulder, splashing the bathroom stall as she climaxed.

"Oh God, oh God, oh God," Jaime whispered, leaning back, breathless, against the door, her breasts heaving, milk making little rivers down her belly, soaking her skirt.

"That was fucking fantastic." Caroline's fingers were slick from being buried in her pussy and she sat back, looking at her friend in delighted wonder.

"Um—" Jaime blushed, crossing her arms over her chest, but she didn't get to finish because the door to the bathroom swung open. Both women froze, wide-eyed, hearing the bang of the door of stall beside them. They covered their mouths, trying not to giggle as Jaime struggled back into her bra, letting Caroline help her with her shirt. By that time, their interrupter was washing up at the sink. They waited for her to leave before slipping out of the stall together.

The women washed their hands, drying them with paper towels. Jaime patted at the waistband of her skirt with paper towel. She'd soaked it with milk.

"I'm all sticky."

Caroline helped her, both women straightening clothes, fixing hair. "We'll eat dinner fast so we can get you home and..." She hesitated, meeting Jaime's bright blue eyes in the mirror, feeling herself flush, seeing the redness creeping into her cheek as she finished her sentence. "Out of those clothes."

Jaime met her eyes and did something that surprised Caroline far more than anything that had happened so far that night. She leaned over and kissed her, soft and sweet and lingering.

"I like that idea," Jaime breathed. Then she smiled, licking her lips. "Mmm. I do taste good!"

"Yeah, you do." Caroline grinned and both women jumped as the bathroom door swung open again.

"Everything okay in here?" Nicki eyed them, frowning. "We were getting worried."

"Fine!" Caroline sang, grabbing Jaime's elbow and steering her toward the door. The last thing she wanted to do was make Sergeant Nicki suspicious. She already looked down on them both for being single mothers. Caroline waggled her fingers as they passed. "See you back at the table."

Caroline's ravioli was as cold as death, but she wasn't hungry anymore anyway and smiled when she realized why—she had a belly full of breast milk. Jaime, on the other hand, was starving. She scarfed down her own fettuccini alfredo and then Caroline's entrée too. They didn't talk at all during the rest of the meal, listening to the other moms complain about carpool and soccer games and husbands who came home late and never helped with the dishes, but all the while, their eyes kept meeting, a secret heat between them.

"We've got another Moms' Night Out scheduled next month at P.F. Chang's," Nicki reminded them as Jaime and Caroline stood to leave. They weren't the first to go— another pair of mothers had left just a few minutes earlier, claiming they both had a nine a.m. soccer games to take kids to—but they had both silently agreed that it was time as soon as the first mothers began to disperse. "Are you two coming? Remember, you have to commit to at least two events a month—"

"We'll let you know," Jaime said, stopping Caroline's unuttered reassurances. "Thanks, everyone, it was fun, but I've gotta get back to my babies before I burst!"

A few of the mothers smiled in understanding, but Nicki rolled her eyes, muttering, "That's what bottles are for, right?" as the two of them started away from the table.

"Don't bother." Caroline squeezed her friend's hand, feeling Jaime tense and start to turn back. "Not worth it."

Back at Jaime's apartment, Caroline paid Jeanie and inquired about how the night went while Jaime slipped into the bedroom to feed the twins. Kyle was asleep on his belly in the Pack 'n Play, thumb stuck firmly in his mouth. He'd kicked his covers off and Caroline covered him up, glancing over at Jaime in the rocking chair, a baby cradled in each arm.

"They sleeping?" Caroline tiptoed over. Jaime smiled, kissing the top of Hannah's nearly-bald blonde head, and then Harry's. They were fraternal twins, but they looked so much alike it was startling.

"Help me put them down?"

Caroline took Hannah—she was the one in the pink and brown sleeper—her belly tightening as she saw Jaime's exposed, milky nipple. She fought her own reaction, chiding herself as she put the baby gently down in the crib. Hannah felt light in her arms. Caroline was used to Kyle's weight, and at a year and a half, he was a hefty little man! Jaime put Harry down next to his sister, and both women smiled at the way the babies sighed and wiggled and stretched until they were touching, side-by-side, probably just as they had been in the womb.

"Thanks for your help." Jaime found Caroline's hand, squeezing gently. "I mean... not just now... but tonight at the restaurant too. Thank you..." Jaime glanced sideways at her friend. "I really don't know what I'd do without you."

Caroline threaded her fingers through hers. "The feeling's pretty mutual, you know."

"Is it?" Jaime turned toward her, face tilted up, gaze soft, lips slightly parted.

"Yeah." Caroline swallowed, glancing over at Kyle sleeping in the playpen. "Listen, I think I'm too drunk to drive home tonight."

"Good." Jaime barely whispered the word before she kissed her, as light and sweet as summer rain, and Caroline found herself tangled in her arms, her hair, their bodies pressed tight and close.

"Jaime," Caroline whispered her name, moaning when her friend's hand cupped her breast through the thin fabric of her blouse. "Oh God..."

"My room." Jaime led the way, turning the light off and the baby monitor on in the nursery. In the dimness of Jaime's bedroom, on the double bed she shared with Rob when he was home on leave, the two of them shoved off all the discarded clothes and the forgotten breast pump so they could roll and rock and moan, stripping each other impatiently down to soft, bare skin.

"Have you ever done this before?" Caroline asked, feeling Jaime's hips moving against hers, their pussies close enough to kiss. The sensation was incredible.

"Nope." Jaime giggled, slipping her thigh over hers. "There's a first time for everything, right?"

Caroline couldn't keep her hands off her, could barely believe this was actually happening. They kissed again, tongues twining, and the feel of Jaime's wetness against her thigh, riding slowly up and down, was making her crazy.

Jaime broke their kiss with a question. "Have you?"

"Yeah," Caroline admitted, flushing.

"So teach me."

Caroline moaned softly, sliding her hand down between Jaime's soft thighs. Her pussy was incredibly swollen and wet, and she opened eagerly, spreading her legs and pushing her hips up to meet Caroline's probing fingers.

"I want to lick you."

"Yes, please." Jaime nodded, her belly quivering as Caroline kissed her way downward, spreading her pussy lips with her fingers first, and then the slow slide of her tongue. Jaime moaned, pulling her knees back, giving her better access, and Caroline took it, her fingers slipping inside as she explored the pink folds of her friend's pussy with her mouth.

Caroline couldn't help touching herself too, rubbing lightly at her clit, teasing, wanting it to go on and on. Jaime mewled and spread and quivered, begging her not to stop, calling out her name, burying her hands in the mass of Caroline's hair. She could have licked her forever, swallowing the musky taste of her juices, letting them nourish her just as she'd taken Jaime's milk earlier.

"Oh fuck!" Jaime rocked faster and Caroline kept her mouth fastened tightly to her friend's sopping pussy, sucking hard on her clit. "Oh! Make me come! Oh make me come in your mouth! All over your face!"

The next moment was heaven as Jaime climaxed, arching her whole body, her nipples hard and pointing straight at the ceiling, exploding with creamy jets of liquid. The bed trembled with her orgasm, and both women cried out in surprise as they found themselves under a pulsing white shower of milk.

"Sorry," Jaime gasped, giggling. "I can't help it. They just do that."

"It's so fucking hot!" Caroline gasped, sliding up to kiss her, licking milk trails along the way.

Jaime shifted her weight, cupping Caroline's breast in her hand. They were smaller than Jaime's—had started out that way—and she wasn't engorged like her friend.

"My turn?"

"Yes. Oh yes." She reclined so Jaime could lick at her coffee-colored nipples. They were so hard they almost hurt and Jaime bathed them with her tongue. "Suck them, hon. Please. Suck them hard."

Jaime did as she was asked, eager to please, and after a moment, gave a sharp gasp, pulling back and looking wide-eyed at her friend.

"Are you still nursing Kyle?"

Caroline smiled. "He hasn't quite weaned yet."

"Wow." Jaime licked her lips. "That's yummy."

"Want some more?" Caroline arched her back and Jaime took her other nipple between her lips, sucking, sucking hard, making Caroline moan and thrust.

Jaime gasped and swallowed, her hand reaching down and finding another surprise between her friend's legs. "You're shaved!"

"Like it?"

"Oh wow." Jaime's eyes got bigger as her fingers explored the baby-soft skin of Caroline's vulva. She gasped when Jaime found her clit, teasing, rubbing. "Now I really want to taste you."

"Are you sure?" The thought made Caroline's pussy clench in anticipation. "You don't have to."

"Yes!" Jaime assured her, already sliding her body south, her sweet mouth seeking heat. "Oh God, it's so smooth!"

"Yesss." Caroline spread her thighs wider, using her fingers to open her pussy lips, showing Jaime exactly where she wanted her mouth. "Here, baby. Right here. Ohhh yes like that. On my clit. Ohhh God."

"Is that okay?" Jaime lapped tentatively at first, then faster, encouraged by Caroline's noises, her movements, the way she grabbed her friend's hair, guiding her mouth just where she wanted—*needed*—it.

"I want your pussy," Caroline begged. "Please. In my mouth."

Jaime lifted her face, glistening with her friend's juices, eyes wide. "But..."

"Come here," Caroline insisted, reaching for her, swinging her friend's hips around.

Jaime straddled her face, looking back, unsure. "Like this?"

"God yes." Caroline wrapped her arms around Jaime's ass, pulling her pussy down to her mouth, devouring her. She was so wet, so sweet, the slick taste in her throat making her crave more. "Oh you taste so good."

Jaime was licking at Caroline's pussy again, spreading her with her fingers. "So do you."

"Don't stop."

"I promise."

They wiggled and writhed on the bed together, faces buried, tongues busy, the soft sound of their moans filling the room. Caroline marveled at the soft lash of the tongue against her clit. For a girl who'd never done it before, Jaime was a quick study, and what she lacked in experience, she made up for in enthusiasm. She didn't want it to ever end, but she was too hot to keep going for much longer. Between the persistent tongue bath between her thighs and the taste and pulse of her friend's pussy in her mouth, she was a goner.

"Oh, Jaime, baby, you're gonna make me come," Caroline moaned, giving up, giving in, letting her hips rise to meet the soft suck of her friend's mouth.

"Me toooo," Jaime cried, and Caroline moaned, feeling the first wave of pleasure rush through her with a tremendous shudder. She grabbed Jaime's ass, plunging her tongue deep, burying her face, feeling the thick pulse of her friend's pussy against her mouth as she climaxed, both of them moaning loudly, not remembering or caring about the babies sleeping right next door.

They collapsed together in a heap on the bed, panting and giggling and rolling, kissing deeply, tasting each other. One of the babies made a soft cry on the monitor and they both stiffened, waiting, but then there was quiet again.

"You're so soft," Jaime marveled, nuzzling her cheek against the side of Caroline's breast.

"Nice, isn't it?"

"The nicest," Jaime agreed, sliding her thigh up over Caroline's. "Mmm, I think I want more."

"Me too." Caroline smiled. "Sit up."

Jaime sat cross-legged on the bed beside her.

"No, here, on top of me." Caroline wrapped her arms around her waist, pulling her close, feeling the delicious weight of her.

"Like this?"

"A little sideways..." Caroline shifted her hips, feeling the wet slide of Jaime's pussy. God, she was wet. It was such a turn-on. "Put your leg between mine... ohhh yes... so we can rub our pussies together."

Jaime gasped in surprise, looking down between their legs. "Ohhh that's really good!"

"I know." Caroline grabbed her friend's hips, guiding her, nice and slow. "That's it. Ride me like that. Ohhhh."

Jaime rocked and rolled, her hips making circles, rubbing her whole pussy round and round, the wetness between them growing. The more excited she got, the harder her nipples and Caroline watched, delighted, as milk began to appear in droplets and then run in little white rivers down her breasts and over her belly.

"Ohhh God." Jaime moaned, her hands gripping Caroline's thighs, biting her lower lip. The sight of her was almost enough to send Caroline over the edge. "That's so fucking good!"

"More, baby," Caroline encouraged, reaching a finger out to catch a droplet of milk from her friend's hard, pink nipple and bringing it to her mouth. "Faster. Come on. Ride me!"

Jaime rocked faster, milk beginning to spurt a little from the motion. Her eyes flew open and she flushed, apologizing. "I'm sorry, I should get a towel."

"Don't you dare!" Caroline grabbed Jaime's breasts, squeezing, sticky white liquid wetting her hands. "I want to milk you. I want you to shower me with it when you come. Will you do that? Come all over me?"

"Yes!" Jaime's eyes lit up. "Oh yes. Oh my pussy feels so good. Pinch them, yes! Milk my titties!"

"Oh fuck! Faster!" Caroline moaned, scissoring her legs with Jaime's, her clit aching, rubbing, wanting. "Do it faster! You're going to make me come!"

"Now!" Jaime arched, slamming her pussy against hers again and again, the trickle of milk from her breasts turning almost instantly into a torrent. "Oh! Ohhh!"

Caroline grabbed Jaime's hips, forcing her pussy against hers, hard and deep, their flesh melding, the sticky wetness making for the perfect orgasm. She bucked on the bed, Jaime's milk spraying her belly, her breasts, even making it into the sweet open "O" of her mouth as she cried out with her climax.

"Holy fuck!" Jaime buried her face in Caroline's neck, both of them sticky with milk and pussy juice. "We need a shower."

"I'll say," Caroline gasped, laughing. "We made a huge mess."

In the other room came the unmistakable sound of one of the babies sucking on a thumb or a fist, reminding them both that Jaime would have to give her milk to the infants they were meant to nourish. Caroline cupped her friend's ass in her hands, reluctant to let her go.

"So what do you think, are we going back to Moms' Night Out?" Jaime asked, up on her elbow so she could meet her eyes.

"Ugh. Do we really need to?" Caroline made a face. "That Nicki is something else."

"Nah." Jaime smiled, tracing a lazy fingernail around Caroline's nipple, making her shiver. "Besides, I think we'll have more fun having a Moms' Night *In* once a month instead."

"You can say that again," Caroline agreed, but Jaime didn't say anything, instead she just leaned in and kissed her, their mouths meeting in a silent, sticky promise for many more nights like this together.

Girl Scout Trip

What can you do with a dozen fourteen-year-old Girl Scouts, three dozen Hershey's chocolate bars, two boxes of graham crackers and four bags of marshmallows when you're thirty miles from any known civilization?

Paige could think of a few things, not the least of which involved going to prison for homicide—those pointy marshmallow sticks would make a great weapon, she mused—but she gritted her teeth and agreed to take them all down to the lake to swim so Brandi could finish setting up camp.

"Are you sure you know how to pitch a tent?" Paige asked doubtfully, watching the other "adult volunteer" in their little band of merrymakers pulling tent poles out of a bag.

Even though Brandi had taken charge once the bus had arrived at the camp site, barking orders clearly enough to get the girls moving, setting up their tents and unpacking their gear, Paige still wasn't quite sure Brandi knew what she was doing, exactly.

Maybe it was her own brunette's natural prejudice against the petite blonde—or maybe it was Brandi's bright idea that using some of the kerosene would help the fire start a little faster. Paige had thankfully made it to the girls before they tried *that* brilliant idea, or all of them would have gone home to their parents without eyebrows.

"I'll be fine!" Brandi blew a stray length of blond hair out of her eyes, sitting back on her heels in her hiking boots. She was wearing her green Girl Scout sash with all her badges, everything from her Brownie wings to her Senior Scout badge and Paige had to resist the urge to make a joke about Girl Scout cookies being made from real Girl Scouts so hard she actually bit her tongue. "Please, just take the girls down to the lake. Let them swim and have fun. I'll finish up here."

"If you're sure?" Paige glanced over at the giggling group of girls, already in their suits, towels slung over their shoulders, among them Paige's little sister, Jess—the sole reason she'd agreed to come along on this exasperating outing in the first place.

"Go!" Brandi insisted, flashing her a very broad smile as she struggled with the tent bag. "I'll have it all fixed up by the time you get back. That's your tent, isn't it?"

"Uh, yeah, but..." Paige looked over at her gear—less than half of what most of the other girls had dragged along. She was a seasoned camper, even if she'd never been a Girl Scout.

"I'll set your tent up too, as payback, okay?" Brandi stood, brushing her hands off on her khaki shorts and shooing Paige toward the waiting gaggle of girls. "Then we can get that fire going and roast hot dogs and marshmallows!"

"Okayyy, but no kerosene, right?" Paige backed away, still doubtful, but there was no arguing with that blinding, over-confident smile and squeaky reassurance. Besides, what trouble could she get into setting up tents, Paige reasoned, directing her charges down the path toward the beach.

The girls were just as obnoxious down at the beach, snapping each other with wet towels, comparing suits, whispering jealously about Jess's impressive cleavage, even at her age. Paige looked at her sister, listening to the other girls with her own painful memories of being teased about her ample bust size, knowing the girl would eventually come to appreciate her bra size. It certainly drew all the boys' attention, that was for sure—although in Paige's case, that had been annoying. For Jess, who didn't have a gay bone in her boy-crazy little body, it would be a boon.

She took out her Kindle and read for an hour while the girls swam and played and generally made a nuisance of themselves. The sun was starting to sink low in the sky and she judged it was about seven. Time to get them all back to camp for dinner. As if on cue, Jess sidled up and started complaining that she was hungry. Paige stowed her Kindle in her beach bag and stood, brushing stand off her cut-offs.

"Let's go then." Paige led the troop back toward camp, up a long hill that had seemed a lot easier on the way down. By the time they got back, they were hot and tired and even hungrier.

Unfortunately, Brandi hadn't made much progress on the fire. In fact, she hadn't made much progress on anything. Brandi's own tent was still flat as a pancake and Paige didn't even see her own. With a sigh, Paige, directed Jess toward the fire, giving her instructions on how to feed it and, making sure the kerosene was well out of reach, she went over to help Brandi.

"Everything okay?" Paige squatted down next to the blonde, who sat in the middle of her flat tent with her knees up, arms crossed, face buried in them. "Need some help?"

"Oh no, I'm fine." Brandi sniffed, lifting her head and wiping at her tear-stained cheeks. "Just peachy. Everything is just grand."

Paige frowned at the blonde's tears. She couldn't fathom the reason for them.

"What happened?"

Brandi sniffed and pointed toward the trees. Paige followed her direction and her gaze fell on something she instantly recognized. It was her own tent, caught high up in a tree, tangled in the branches.

"How in the hell...?" She blinked in surprise, looking back at Brandi, trying not to throttle her.

"I'm sooo sorry," Brandi wailed, burying her face in her hands. Her words were muffled and interrupted intermittently by sobs. "The wind took it! I ran after it, but I couldn't catch it in time. And then... and then..."

"Then?" Paige prompted, staring at her tent caught in the tree, seeing the giant hole in the side that definitely shouldn't have been there.

"Then I tried to get it down," Brandi wailed. "I tried climbing and I did this!"

She held up her hands, ripped to shreds by the bark.

"And then I fell and did this." Brandi turned her leg to the side, showing her a decent sized gash on the side. "So I tried using the tent poles, but they got caught. And then… your tent ripped…"

Paige watched as the girl started sobbing again, uncontrollably this time. She was clearly, completely overwhelmed and the other girls were starting to notice. Without their fearless leader, Paige feared they would have anarchy on their hands. Besides, while Brandi clearly had bitten off more than she could chew with this trip, she didn't deserve to be sitting in the middle of the woods crying about a ripped tent and a lackluster campfire.

"Okay," Paige soothed, putting her hand on the girl's arm. "It's okay. We'll fix it."

"Paige, I'm starving!" Jess skipped over toward them, complaining the whole way.

"Jess, listen." Paige stood, screening her view of the sobbing Brandi. "Go in the cooler and get the hot dogs. You and the girls start cooking, okay? I'm going to help Brandi get her tent up and we'll be right there."

Jess cocked her head, frowning, but she didn't question her sister's instructions.

"Come on," Paige said, holding out her hand to the blonde. Brandi's nose was red from crying, her cheeks streaked with dirt. "Let's get your tent set up."

It didn't take them long, with Paige's instruction, to get the little two-man pup tent up. It wasn't as nice as Paige's, but it also didn't have a giant hole ripped in the side. She didn't know what she was going to do without a tent all weekend, but she'd cross that bridge later.

"I'm really, really sorry about your tent." Brandi looked mournfully up into the tree. "I'll pay you back for it."

"Do you have a first-aid kit in here?" Paige asked, going through Brandi's gear.

"Of course," she scoffed, holding her hand out for the bag. "Here."

Paige handed it over and Brandi produced a hard-backed first-aid kit complete with a red cross on the front and a Girl Scout logo in the corner.

"What are you doing?" Brandi asked as Paige crawled into the two-man tent.

"Get in here," Paige called.

"I'm so sorry." Brandi crawled in, dragging her gear and sleeping bag behind her. Paige waited for her to roll out her sleeping bag and get on top of it. "You can have my tent and sleeping bag tonight if you want. I can sleep by the fire."

"I don't want to have to put you out in the middle of the night." Paige snorted, grabbing the blonde's calf and yanking it toward her.

Brandi yelped in surprise, half sitting, half-laying as Paige inspected the wound on her leg. It was long but not deep and Paige opened the first-aid box, sorting through it for what she needed.

"I'm not an idiot," Brandi said, wincing when Paige dabbed the cut with hydrogen peroxide.

"I know," Paige soothed, blowing gently on the other girl's gashed leg. It was a very nice leg, Paige had to admit, and she was sorry to see it wounded. "But you haven't exactly made the best camping decisions so far this trip, you know?"

"I just thought the kerosene would help things along," Brandi protested, her voice small as she watched Paige drying the cut with the heat of her breath. "And I said I was sorry about the tent."

"I know you are." Paige smiled at her, trying to be encouraging. Given the amount of badges on the girl's uniform, she had to know a *little* something about camping, she reasoned. Maybe Brandi was just having a bad day. Or week. "It's okay. I'm just glad you're still in once piece."

Paige put a large Band-Aid over the cut, smoothing it gently over the other girl's skin. Her legs were incredibly soft and shapely, even in hiking boots. Maybe especially in hiking boots. She felt the warm rush of arousal when she realized, with Brandi sitting like that, knees up and legs open, she could see right down the leg of khaki shorts. She was wearing white panties with little cherries on them.

"Thanks for your help," Brandi said softly and when Paige glanced at her, she saw the girls had tears still brimming and her lower lip trembled. "I guess I'm not as good at all of this as I thought."

"Sure you are." Paige cleared her throat, picking up the Band-Aid wrappers and busying herself putting everything back into the first-aid kit. "You're doing fine."

"You're a bad liar." Brandi sniffed and then laughed, swiping at her tears.

"Probably." Paige grinned. "The good news is, I'm here, and I *do* know what I'm doing."

"Well at least that makes one of us." Brandi smiled back. "Oh my God, do I smell hot dogs? I'm starving."

"I had the girls start cooking." Paige snapped the first aid kit closed. "Let's go eat."

Brandi rolled over and started crawling out of the tent, giving Paige a very nice view of her pleasingly rounded rump on the way out. That isn't what you're here for, she reminded herself, as she followed Brandi out of the tent. It had been months since she'd been with anyone—almost six since Paige's last girlfriend, Susan, had moved to Arizona with her family. They'd tried the long distance thing, but it hadn't worked out so well, especially after Susan had found a pretty blonde Barbie to hang out with.

Blondes had never been Paige's type, but she couldn't help watching the pretty blonde across the fire, balancing her hot dog on the end of a stick. The younger girls were giggling and talking about boys like typical tweens and Paige noticed Brandi abstaining from the conversation. Of course, that didn't mean anything. It most definitely didn't indicate that she liked girls instead of boys, she told herself, tearing apart a Ballpark frank and popping the end into her mouth.

There was no point getting her hopes up. Besides, she couldn't risk it. She could see the headlines—*Leader Assaulted by Lesbian on Girl Scout Trip*. Paige didn't need any more drama. Susan had been drama enough, and she had been a mousy little girl with brown hair and glasses, very nerdy and studious—until you got her into bed. Then she turned from mouse into lioness on the prowl.

Paige warmed at the memory, feeling her face filling with heat. When she glanced across the fire, she saw Brandi putting marshmallows on sticks for the girls with a little smile on her face. Their eyes met and Paige could have sworn the corners of her mouth turned up a little more at the corners in response.

"Here, do mine." Jess handed over her marshmallow and stick in frustration. Paige shoved the pillowy marshmallow onto the stick and handed it back to her sister, licking the stickiness from her fingers, watching Brandi do the same across the flames.

When the girls started singing camp fire songs, Paige decided she wasn't up for any more cheerful Girl Scoutness and excused herself. She just wanted to curl up, pull her sleeping back over her head, and forget all the paths her brain seemed to want to travel tonight, because that way led to disaster. She was sure of it.

Paige found her gear and started untying her sleeping bag. The ground was soft with pine needles under her feet. She decided, instead of putting her sleeping bag inside Brandi's tent and risk temptation, to spread it out under the stars. The moon was full, providing plenty of light, even as the fire was beginning to wane. She undressed down to her underwear and t-shirt, glancing over at the girls, wondering if she should remind them to put out the fire before they all went to sleep.

Brandi will handle it, she told herself. The night air was cool and she hurried into her sleeping bag, zipping it all the way up and closing her eyes. The crickets sang along with the girls, a Girl Scout nature lullaby, but Paige had a hard time falling asleep, although she was exhausted from all the hiking and carrying and babysitting.

She kept thinking of Brandi smiling at her through her tears, and how the girl's calf had felt in her palm, so soft and supple. And those damnable panties covered in little red cherries. Paige didn't know how long it took, but by the time Brandi came back to her tent, she was sleeping soundly.

She never would have woken up at all of Brandi hadn't tripped over her. They both swore out loud as Brandi sprawled over Paige in the moonlight, landing full force, knocking the wind out of both of them. Paige popped her head out of her sleeping bag, blinking and trying to make sense of where she was. It took several moments before she remembered she was in the middle of the woods on her little sister's Girl Scout trip.

"What are you doing out here?" Brandi whispered, her body still on top of Paige.

"Sleeping," Paige replied, stating the obvious, wondering if it was hard to breathe because Brandi's full weight was on her, or if was more the way the blonde squirmed on top.

"Why aren't you in the tent?"

"It's not my tent," Paige reminded her. "Mine's in a tree, remember?"

"I said I was sorry." Brandi sighed and rolled off, sitting on the bed of pine needles between the sleeping bag and the tent.

"Are the girls sleeping?"

"All tucked in." Brandi yawned and stretched and, as Paige's eyes adjusted to the light, she saw how her shirt rode up, exposing an expanse of her belly.

"You put the fire out?" Paige hated herself for asking but it was better safe than sorry.

"Of course," Brandi scoffed.

"You sent one of the girls down to the lake for water?" Paige sat up, pushing her sleeping bag down to her waist, already knowing the answer by Brandi's hesitation.

"...well, no..."

"I'll do it." Paige sighed, climbing out of her sleeping bag and hunting around for her backpack with her jeans in it.

"No, it's fine. I'll do it." Brandi stood in a huff, already heading toward the lake.

Without a flashlight. Or anything to bring water back with.

Paige rolled her eyes, swearing under her breath as she found a flashlight in her bag, grabbing her empty water bottle and putting on a pair of crocs before heading after her. Brandi was practically running and Paige didn't want to go too fast, considering she was only wearing crocs. And no pants, she realized, halfway down the path to the lake.

When she reached the beach, she waved her flashlight around, looking for Brandi. The lake was quiet, the moon shining on the water, but there was no sign of life.

"Guess who?"

Paige gasped as Brandi covered her eyes with her hands, her breath warm against her cheek, her lips tickling Paige's ear, making goose bumps rise up on her arms.

"Jesus, you scared the crap out of me." Paige could barely get the words out and Brandi giggled.

"Come on, the girls are asleep." Brandi's voice had lowered to a bare whisper, as if anyone could hear them, way out here. "Let's go skinny dipping."

Skinny dipping?

Paige had barely registered the concept before Brandi stepped out from behind her, already stripped naked and heading for the water. She stood, rooted to the spot, watching the girl's blonde hair fly out behind her as she ran toward the shoreline, her legs long and pale in the moonlight, her breasts tiny, pert. Perfect.

Hesitating only a moment, Paige pulled her t-shirt off, then slid her panties down, leaving them along with her water bottle and flashlight in the sand and following Brandi to the edge of the water. She was still wading in. Paige expected the water to be cold, but the day had been so hot, it was as warm as bath water.

"Oh this feels soooo good!" Brandi moaned as she waded in to her waist. Paige could still see her breasts, more fully now, the tips hard and pointing straight at her.

"Water's warm." Paige waded in too, feeling Brandi's gaze on her body, wondering what she was thinking. Paige was far curvier—and bustier—than the blonde. Probably thinks I'm fat, Paige thought, sinking lower in the water, eager to hide her full hips.

"It's heaven," Brandi agreed, spreading her arms and falling back, floating on the surface. "Look at the stars!"

Paige let herself go, floating on her back on the still surface of the lake. Above them, a million stars and a bright, full moon looked down. Below them, a lake teeming with life. Paige breathed deeply, wishing everything could be like this, so uncomplicated, so beautiful. There were no words between them, but the silence wasn't awkward. Paige felt something, like the heavy air before a storm started, between the two of them.

She felt it, when their bodies floated together. Brandi's calf brushed hers. Then her hip. Then her hand. Paige held her breath, listening to the soft sound of waves lapping the shoreline, feeling Brandi's hand caress her thigh. It was a light, gentle, rhythmic touch but definitely purposeful. Brandi was stroking her leg. Paige tried not to react but her nipples were hard and the aching throb between her legs was very distracting.

"Brandi?" Paige swallowed, not even sure what to ask, how to begin.

"Hm?" That soft hand, lapping at her thigh, like the water licking the shoreline.

"Are you... do you...?" She couldn't seem to finish a sentence.

"Mmmm hmmmm." Brandi's fingers tiptoed into the V of her thighs, fingers warm, probing, making Paige gasp and then moan softly. "Ohhh smooth. Like me. Want to feel?"

There was no question anymore in Paige's mind or on her lips. Her own hand drifted over to Brandi's thigh, marveling at the softness of her skin before seeking even more heat. She came up against no resistance at all. Brandi's thighs parted sweetly and Paige's fingers stroked her slit—smooth and soft, just as promised—hearing her sharp intake of breath.

"Do little circles." Brandi whispered her instructions, her own fingers showing Paige, finding her clit, rubbing it around and around.

"Oh God." Paige shivered, her pussy throbbing, her clit eager for more. She rubbed Brandi too, her labia swelling under the attention.

"Like that," Brandi gasped, hips rocking up with the current. "Oh yes, like that!"

Paige wanted to grab the girl and bury her face in her pussy. She wanted to taste her, drink her, eat her until Brandi bucked and moaned and came in her mouth. But she didn't want Brandi to stop touching her. The fingers between her legs, rubbing fast and furious against her clit, were skilled and too good to deny. Brandi was going to get her off right here while they both floated together on the surface of the lake.

"Mmmmm don't stop," Brandi urged, making those same circles with her hips, urging her on. "Ohhhhh fuckkk don't stop! You're going to make me come!"

Paige moaned, thrusting up against those persistent fingertips, trying to focus on giving her pleasure while her own body was so tightly wound and ready to take off, like a delicious rocket. Brandi cried out, back arching, as she came, her breath coming almost as fast as her fingers moving on Paige's throbbing clit.

And then Paige took off, rocketing skyward, hard nipples pointed to the stars as a climax rocked her body with the waves. Her pussy clamped down, spasming with pleasure, a release so sudden it shocked her. She shuddered with her orgasm, feeling Brandi's pussy still pulsing under her own fingers, making her mouth water. God, she wanted her. Still. More.

"Ohhhh God that felt so good." Brandi sighed happily, lifting her fingers to her mouth. Paige's pussy, still pulsing from her climax, spasmed in response. "Now I want to taste you."

Was she dreaming? Paige thought she must be dreaming. She was still cocooned in her sleeping bag and Brandi was snoring in the tent beside her. She was sure of it until the blonde beside her uprighted herself, grabbing Paige around the waist, pulling her upright too. She thought they would sink, that they must be miles from the shore, but they were still in shallow water. When Paige put her feet down on the rocks, her breasts were still above the water line.

Brandi eyed them with a curious hunger and before she knew it, Paige's nipple was in the blonde's mouth. She gasped in surprise, hanging into the slighter girl as she wrapped her legs around Paige, hooking her heels behind her calves. Brandi's mouth was hot on her cool skin, the girl's hands wandering all over Paige's curves like she couldn't get enough.

Then Brandi's head came up and their mouths met, melted, slanting hot and insistent, hands roaming. Paige let her hands roam too, lifting the other girl with both hands gripping her ass. Brandi squealed and laughed as they fell back into the water with a splash, both of them coming up sputtering.

"Come on, let's go back," Brandi urged and Paige felt her heart drop. Was it over then? Just a little bit of fun in the water?

But Brandi grabbed her hand, dispelling that idea. "I still want to taste you."

Paige actually remembered what they'd gone down to the lake for and filled her water bottle before they put their t-shirts on and started walking back up the path, the flashlight bobbing in the dark. Brandi was barefoot and she scoffed at Paige's insistence she put on shoes but gave up halfway down the path.

"Here, get on." Paige hunkered down and let Brandi climb onto her back. She carried her that way, piggyback, to camp. She dropped Brandi at the tent, whispering, "I'll be right back."

There was no sound from the girls' tents, no late-night flashlights left on. Paige quickly poured water over the fire, hearing the embers give their last hiss, before heading back to her own tent. Well, Brandi's tent. She took her crocs off and left them outside, unzipping the flap and crawling in. Brandi had her sleeping bag spread out flat on the bottom, soft side up. She'd taken off her t-shirt and smiled at Paige as she entered the tent.

Paige thought she'd never seen anything more beautiful in her life. The blonde was on her back, knees up and open, leaning back on her elbows, a hungry look in her eyes. Paige took the time to zip the tent up against mosquitos before she turned and dove between Brandi's open legs, making her squeal and giggle.

"Shhh!" Paige insisted, her head coming up. "Don't wake the girls."

Brandi nodded, biting her lip as Paige nuzzled the soft skin between her legs, parting her labia with her eager tongue. She tasted like the lake, her skin cool from their swim and the night air, but that didn't last long. Paige lapped at her flesh, using her tongue to part her slit, sliding it down and then up again, over and over, feeling her squirm.

"Here," Brandi urged, nudging her clit with her index finger.

Paige's tongue made circles around her clit, nuzzling her nose into her swelling mound. The taste and smell of her was intoxicating. It made her own pussy throb with need. Brandi seemed to sense this because she wiggled and turned and squirmed and situated herself so she could wrap her arms around Paige's hips and pull her pussy against her mouth.

"Oh fuck," Paige gasped when Brandi's lips fastened over her mound, her tongue making fast circles around and around her clit. She knew it was Brandi's way of showing her what she wanted, and Paige mimicked her movement with her own tongue, hearing a satisfying moan escape her lips.

Paige tried to keep quiet, not wanting anyone to hear them, but Brandi's mouth was so good it was hard to keep from crying out. She kept her mouth busy between Brandi's soft, slender thighs, pussy juice wet against her cheeks. Paige wanted to explore every inch of her and slipped her fingers between her lips, tracing that sweet, slippery labyrinth. Brandi wriggled and thrust up when she slid two fingers inside. She was like a soft, velvet purse, walls quivering and hugging Paige's fingers.

She gasped when Brandi did the same, sliding two fingers into Paige's quivering pussy. They mirrored each other, tongues lapping, circling, fingers moving slowly in and out at first, then faster, deeper, plunging home. Paige couldn't concentrate anymore, the pleasure so intense, building to a fever pitch. She felt her impending orgasm—it trembled her thighs like an earthquake.

Then Brandi was coming all over her face, hips thrusting up toward the sky, and Paige's climax rocked through her at the same time, like a freight train. Her whole body convulsed with pleasure, her pussy snapping closed on Brandi's plunging fingers again and again. Paige moaned into Brandi's sweet, pink flesh, mashing her whole face against her mound until she couldn't breathe and didn't care. She wanted to drown in her.

"No more! No more!" It was Brandi who gasped and pushed her off, clamping her hand protectively over her swollen mound.

"Mmmmmore." Paige turned and crawled up to kiss her on the mouth, their saliva and juices a heady mix. "Jesus, that was fucking hot. Where did that even come from?"

Brandi smiled lazily, snaking an arm around her neck and pulling Paige down to her. Paige grabbed the edge of the sleeping bag and covered them both, cocooning them in the darkness. They were quiet for a while, watching fireflies light up outside the tent, listening to the sound of crickets and frogs.

"This is so wrong," Paige murmured as Brandi snuggled up, using her ample breasts as pillows. "My little sister is just over there."

Brandi snorted. "It was your little sister who told me..."

"She told you?" Paige blinked at the sloping V at the top of the tent, thinking about her own, caught up in a tree. Jess had planned this? The little stinker! She'd acted all innocent! "Wait a minute... my tent! Did you do that on purpose?"

"No!" Brandi laughed, shaking her head. "Although... now I'm kind of glad I messed up so bad."

"You didn't mess up." Paige smiled, closing her eyes and breathing in the sweet, fragrant smell of her hair, like corn silk against her nose. "In fact, I'm pretty sure you just earned another merit badge."

"Oh yeah? What for?"

Paige grinned, sliding her hand over Brandi's still-slick mound, making her giggle and squirm. "Here, let me show you."

Pool Party

Nancy didn't know what her neighbor had against clothing, but she rarely saw her wearing any. Not that she could blame the woman. Santa Barbara was hot in the summer, and if Nancy looked like the woman next door—a tall, busty, long-legged redhead—she might go around naked all the time too.

They met over their shared fence, a tall, synthetic privacy affair overgrown on Nancy's side with a thick vine of morning glories. One Saturday afternoon, while Nancy was on her hands and knees, wearing her summer uniform of denim shorts and a tank-tee, up to her elbows in dirt digging in her garden, she heard a voice coming from next door.

"I'm pretty sure it's old blue jeans."

Nancy looked up to see her new neighbor's pretty green eyes framed by straight, blunt-cut copper-colored bangs peeking over the fence line.

"Excuse me?" Nancy brushed a stray strand of dark hair out of her eyes, tilting her gardening hat back and peering up at the woman.

"That song you were singing. *Crocodile Rock*, right? Elton John?"

Nancy flushed. She hadn't even realized she was singing.

"It's not Ovaltines, it's blue jeans." The redhead giggled. "'Dreaming of my Chevy and my old blue jeans…' not 'my Ovaltines.'"

"Oh." Nancy blushed a deeper red. "I had no idea."

"I'm Gina, by the way. Gina Cole. I don't think we've met."

Nancy did the polite thing, abandoning her spade and gardening gloves and walking over to the fence to properly introduce herself.

"Nancy. Nancy Weimer. Well, Robbins, once the divorce is final."

The redhead raised one perfectly arched eyebrow. "Would you like condolences or congratulations?"

Nancy laughed. "A little bit of both, I guess. You know how it is."

"Oh, no. Not me." Gina waggled the fingers of her left hand as proof. "Free as a little birdie."

"Well, Santa Barbara is a great place to be young and single."

"Yes it is! I can't say I miss L.A. at all." Gina cocked her head, contemplating her neighbor's garden. "You know, your yard would be just perfect with a pool."

Nancy laughed. "Sorry, inside joke. My husband was a scuba diver. Loved the water. We had a pool. I had it filled in last year and planted this garden."

"Oh, a victory garden!" Gina exclaimed with a giggle.

"Something like that."

Gina jerked her head in the direction of the pool behind her. "Well if you ever get hot, feel free to come on over and hop in my pool. Plenty of room!"

"Thanks." Nancy glanced over her shoulder at where her own pool used to be, where Neil would spend hours doing laps back and forth. "Would you like something from my garden?"

"Organic?" Gina inquired with a frown. "I only eat organic…"

Nancy scoffed, going over and picking a cucumber off one of the trellises. "Of course. These are huge this year."

"My goodness! They certainly are!" The redhead's eyes widened as Nancy handed her the long, fat vegetable. "Well, thank you. I can think of lots of good uses for this guy!"

She smiled. "Welcome to the neighborhood."

Nancy noticed, when Gina reached over the fence, her neighbor was bare-shouldered, but the fence was in the way and she couldn't see any more. It wasn't until the following week, standing on the balcony outside her bedroom window in a robe, towel-drying her hair and looking down at the fence she'd had installed around her garden boxes—the rabbits had eaten all of her new melons—when Nancy saw Gina stretched out beside her pool on a lounge chair wearing absolutely nothing. Well, that wasn't quite true—she had on a floppy white hat and a pair of sunglasses, but that was all.

The fence was tall and afforded plenty of privacy, but houses on their street were smashed together in little squares like postage stamps. California land was at a premium and having more of it was very expensive. Nancy could see everyone's yard on all sides. She stood looking out her window, wondering if the thought had occurred to her new neighbor, who was completely exposed, not only to the elements, but to the eyes of every surrounding neighbor who happened to glance out an upstairs window. Mr. Desoto on the other side of her would certainly be thrilled—the old geezer had flirted with Nancy since she and Neil had moved in as newlyweds. He was probably foaming at the mouth at the sight of their shared neighbor. Thankfully, there were no kids in the neighborhood, at least within sight distance.

What didn't occur to Nancy, as she gaped at her neighbor's admittedly gorgeous nude body, was Gina might be able to see her too—not until Gina leaned over, picking up a drink with an umbrella stuck into it and raising it in Nancy's direction in a salute. Her mouth went instantly dry and her stomach dropped to her toes, having been caught peeping on her neighbor in the raw.

What else could she do but raise a hand in a wave?

The next time they saw each other was one of the few times Nancy saw her neighbor with her clothes on. Gina was wearing a white linen pants suit and heels, with a lemon yellow scarf at her neck and the same floppy white hat, walking two very large but very well-mannered black and white spotted Great Danes past Nancy's yard. Nancy grew as many plants in her front yard as her back one, using the space to cultivate the useful but still pretty flowered ones like lavender, lemongrass, chives, thyme and even curry.

When Nancy waved, Gina stopped to talk, both dogs heeling and sitting at her commands, their big tongues hanging low as they panted on the sidewalk. The women chatted about the dogs (Nancy admitted she was a cat person, owning three of them) and the weather (in Santa Barbara, there hardly was such a thing to discuss, it was always beautiful) and Mr. Desoto (who had, indeed, propositioned his new neighbor) and that, of course, gave Nancy the perfect opportunity to inquire.

"You know, if I can see you sunbathing from my window, Mr. Desoto probably can too?"

Gina rolled her eyes and waved her hand in dismissal. "Let him look. What do I care? I've been in Playboy twice. He can drool over me in the September 2000 issue to his heart's content."

That's when her new neighbor revealed her profession as a model, sometimes actress, and one-time Playboy bunny, and Nancy began to understand her lack of modesty.

"Besides, it's my own backyard," Gina huffed. "I'll do what I like. That's what fences are for."

Nancy nodded. "Good fences make good neighbors."

And that's where they left it.

The next time Nancy saw her new neighbor, Gina was masturbating.

The sight was so shocking, Nancy forgot what she was doing, the fly-swatter in her hand, the one with which she'd been chasing an errant bee around in her room, dropping to the floor. The door to her balcony was open, the screen letting in a nice, cool breeze on a warm summer day, and a honeybee from her hive out back had found its way in through a hole in the screen. But when Nancy saw what her neighbor was doing, all thoughts about the wayward insect were forgotten.

Gina was naked on her lounge chair—a sight Nancy had grown used to, in some ways—her body slick with oil, her skin the color of café au lait. A redhead without freckles was unusual enough, but a redhead with such a rich, beautiful tan was stunning. And she was clearly a "real" redhead, because the hair between the woman's long, slender thighs was a fiery copper color—what there was of it. Below a little triangle at the very top, the woman was completely shaved. Nancy could see that clearly enough, even though Gina's hand, moving between her legs, partially covered the view.

Nancy told herself to walk away, to go back to reading about sustainable gardening and forget about her neighbor's slick, glistening, oiled-up flesh show. But she didn't. She couldn't. She was frozen in place, paralyzed by the arousing sight and sound of the woman's pleasure. The breeze carried Gina's little mews and soft cries as her fingers moved faster between her open thighs.

Nancy couldn't remember how long it had been since she herself had masturbated—since she'd thought about sex at all. With Neil, sex had become such a power struggle, once he was gone, she'd thrown the baby out with the bath water. So to speak. But just the sight of Gina on display, touching herself without reserve—did she know Nancy was watching? That anyone could be watching?—made her clench every muscle she had below the waist.

Don't. Shouldn't. Can't. All the negatives going through her mind made what she was doing—standing in front of the window, legs squeezed tight together, breathing shallow and fast—somehow even more exciting. Nancy couldn't see her neighbor's eyes—her sunglasses were on, and her hat cast half her face in shadow—but she could see her mouth, how she drew her lower lip between her teeth as her hand moved faster and faster between her legs.

Nancy found her own hand wandering south, the denim of her jean shorts too tight, tugging between her thighs. She rubbed the seam, working it into her cleft as she watched her neighbor's gloriously oiled up, tanned, pink-tipped breasts moving with her masturbatory motion, Gina's fingers weren't just rubbing anymore, but plunging deep, fucking herself. Her knees were drawn up, her red-painted toes curled, hips moving up and down on the lounge chair.

What was she imagining? Nancy wondered, leaning against the doorframe as she unzipped her cutoffs and slid her hand into the moist crotch of her panties. Oh fuck, she was wet. She hadn't been wet like this in ages, couldn't remember the last time she'd been aroused at all, in fact. Aside from a few vague wet dreams here or there that burned away in the heat of the day, her life had become so singular and sterile—home, work, garden. The only mating going on in her life had been crossbreeding her plants.

But she was aroused now. Her pussy sucked her fingers in, hungry and desperate for more. It was hardly enough. Nancy remembered something as she watched her neighbor's display, her fingers, three of them—no, four, practically her whole hand!—thrusting in and out of her wet hole, and bolted to her dresser. In the bottom drawer were her pantyhose, slips, a few bits of lingerie from Victoria's Secret to tempt Neil back in the day, and a pink, silicone Rabbit vibrator he had purchased for her one Valentine's Day.

She'd only ever used it once, and when she turned it on, she was sure nothing would happen, that the batteries would not only be dead, but corroded inside—a bit like she felt— and the moment would be gone, everything spoiled. But instead it buzzed to life, sending an exciting jolt through her as she rushed back to the window to watch her neighbor's show, afraid she might have missed the fireworks ending.

But no, Gina was still fucking herself, mouth open now, head back, thigh muscles taut with effort. Nancy flushed, hot and ashamed of herself, but she yanked her shorts and panties off and shoved the vibrator up inside her throbbing pussy with complete abandon, not caring anymore. She was too desperate for an orgasm, watching Gina working toward hers. The vibrator hummed, the silicone rabbit hitting her clitoris at just the right angle, making her moan softly, her nipples hardening under her t-shirt.

"Oh fuck!" Gina cried, hips bucking up fast, hard, again and again. Her words were clear, if a little faint. "Ooooo yeah! Fuck yeah! I'm gonna come!"

Oh.

Oh!

Oh!

Nancy fucked herself with the toy, her level of arousal so high she knew it wouldn't be long before her own orgasm. The hot buzzing between her legs drove her mad with lust and her knees weakened and buckled as she watched her neighbor's climax, the way Gina drove her hips toward the sky as she came and came, her body shuddering with it.

Nancy came too, so suddenly she cried out with the force of it as her orgasm shook her like a livewire, hot, electric, throbbing jolts of pleasure jerking her limbs and making the muscles of her pussy clamp down on the vibrator again and again. Trembling and breathless, she collapsed onto the floor in front of the door, sliding the vibrator out of her still quivering pussy and turning it off.

She didn't peek to see if Gina had heard her, although some part of her wanted to. Instead she rested, catching her breath, feeling the soft touch of the breeze and the warm caress of the sunshine coming through the door wall, wondering how in the hell she had managed so long without *that*. When she had finally recovered, she dared to look over at her neighbor's yard, but the lounge chair was empty. Gina was gone.

Nancy didn't see her again for a few weeks, when Gina stopped on her way by with the dogs as Nancy knelt in the front yard, pruning. Her neighbor tapped her shoulder—she had been so lost in her own thoughts, she hadn't heard her approach—and when Nancy turned and saw who it was, she was sure she blushed as pink as the buds Gina exclaimed over.

"I've never seen such gorgeous roses!"

"These are just ornamental," Nancy explained, trying to hide her flush under the brim of her had. "I like the wild ones out back more. I gather the rosehips in the fall. They're so rich in Vitamin C, you can actually treat colds and flu with them. And I make rose oil out of the seeds. It's a great treatment for wrinkles."

"Really?" The redhead leaned over the roses to breathe in the scent. "I'd like to try some."

"You don't have any wrinkles," Nancy remarked, and it was true, for the most part. Gina seemed ageless, like a long-legged, fiery goddess.

"You're sweet." Gina laughed. "How old would you guess I am?"

"Twenty-eight?" Nancy was twenty-eight.

"Ha. I'm thirty-four." Gina took off her sunglasses, leaning in so close Nancy could smell her perfume, something flowery and sweet, a far better scent than roses. "See these wrinkles? Ugh! Thank god for airbrushing!"

Nancy shook her head. "I don't see anything."

"You're really too sweet." Gina put her sunglasses back on. "Do you have any of that rose oil?"

"Sure." Nancy had made dozens of bottles of the stuff. "I can bring some over later."

"That'd be great!" Gina sighed as one of the dogs at her feet whined and pawed at the leg of her pant suit. Nancy had never seen anyone dress as well as her neighbor. She wore linen and heels to walk the dogs, for Pete's sake! Nancy felt like a drudge in her cut-offs and t-shirt. "Well, I'd better get these beasts their daily exercise."

Nancy looked, but couldn't find any more rose oil in her medicine cabinet. She'd made so much that first winter she could barely store it all, but after Neil moved out, things got so shuffled around, she couldn't remember where she might have put it. It wasn't until the following day, just when she was closing up the flower shop, the day's last wedding bouquets, funeral flowers and I'm-sorry, get-well or I-love-you roses delivered, that she remembered where she'd put them.

All three cats—two fat orange ones named Butch Cassidy and the Sundance Kid (Butch and Sunny for short, Neil's idea) and a slim, gold-eyed, black goddess named

Isis—met her at the door, threading their way around her feet as she tossed her purse and keys on the sideboard. They followed her into the basement, a damp, dark cave where Neil had kept his drum set, through the furnace room. There was a small refrigerator plugged in back there, and she'd forgotten she put all her oils and some of her seeds in there when Neil moved out.

When she knocked on her neighbor's front door, there was no answer, although the dogs barked like mad, pawing and scratching and howling at her. Gina's car was in the driveway, and she wondered if she might be out back, in the pool, where she seemed to spend most of her time. Nancy wandered around the side of the house. It was far larger than her own, three stories instead of just two. Modeling clearly paid better than being a florist.

"Hello?" Nancy called when she reached the gate. It was closed and locked. "Gina? It's Nancy. Are you out here? I brought the rose oil…"

"Hi there, neighbor." Gina smiled, unlatching the gate from the inside and waving her in.

Considering the times she'd seen the woman sunbathing in the nude, Nancy shouldn't have been shocked to find her completely naked, but she was anyway. Gina's whole body seemed to defy gravity. Her self-proclaimed age was thirty-four, but she had the body of a twenty-four year old. As far as Nancy could see, the photographers wouldn't have to do much airbrushing.

Averting her gaze, Nancy held the paper bag up to her neighbor. "Here."

"Thank you!" Gina took the bag, peering inside like a kid opening a present on Christmas. "How much do I owe you?"

"Oh, no." Nancy waved the offer away. "Nothing."

"So how does this work?" Gina held the bottle up in the sunlight, squinting it at, while Nancy tried to look anywhere else besides the pink-tipped curve of her neighbor's breasts and the fiery V between her legs. She couldn't help remembering watching Gina touch herself, and the thought made Nancy feel warmly uncomfortable.

"Just rub a little on the affected area." Nancy cleared her throat. "Corner of the eyes and mouth, you know…"

Gina opened the bottle, shaking a drop onto her finger and taking off her sunglasses before rubbing the oil under her eyes. "Ahhh. There. Wrinkles gone?"

Nancy laughed. "It's not magic. It will take a week or two."

"Oh! Speaking of a week or two!" Gina dropped the bottle back in the bag, putting her sunglasses back on. "I'm having a pool party next weekend and I want you to come."

"Oh, no…" Nancy shook her head. "I don't swim…"

"I insist. Lots of food and fun." Gina pursed her lips for a moment, cocking her head, contemplative. "I think you need to get out, meet people. Lots of hot, eligible men will be invited, I promise."

"I'm not ready for men yet. My divorce isn't even officially final," Nancy reminded her.

It had dragged on two years, a strangely long, protracted affair, given there were no children and there was very little property, but it had taken her a year to track him down in the first place, living somewhere in Florida with the twenty-year-old he'd run off with.

"Men." Gina sighed. "It's enough to make you want to switch teams sometimes, isn't it?"

Nancy just blinked at her. "I really shouldn't…"

"Oh yes you should!" Gina insisted. "If you say no, I'm just going to come over and get you, so you might as well say yes."

"Well maybe." Nancy looked at her neighbor's pool so she wouldn't have to look at her neighbor. The woman's lack of self-consciousness was disconcerting. "I guess I can get someone else to run the shop and do the wedding deliveries." There were always a bunch of those on the weekend.

"Florist or bridal shop?" Gina mused, answering her own question before Nancy could even open her mouth. "Florist. You and plants have a thing."

Nancy smiled. "Yes."

"Well come on, get undressed, we'll go for a swim!" Gina offered, putting the paper bag on a table with her umbrella drink and nodding toward the pool.

"Oh, no!" Nancy protested, glancing up, first at her own house, where her bedroom balcony was in clear view, then the other way, where the neighbor on the other side must also have an unobstructed view from the bedroom window. "Besides, Mr. Desoto."

Gina grinned, coming over to stand so close to Nancy, she could feel the heat radiating from the woman's body in waves, leaning in so she could whisper, "We can put on a good show. Give him a heart attack."

Nancy laughed in spite of her embarrassment, taking a step away. "No, I really have to go."

"Okay." Gina shrugged, and the look of disappointment on her face made Nancy feel strangely guilty for not taking her up on the offer to go for a swim. "Thanks again for the magical rose wrinkle cream!"

Nancy laughed again, opening the gate.

"And you *are* coming next week, I'm not taking no for an answer!" Gina insisted, following her.

"All right," Nancy relented, with Gina right behind her, and that's when her neighbor leaned in and kissed her cheek. It was just a sweet gesture, but the soft feel of her lips, the press of Gina's full, bare breast against her arm, made Nancy feel faint, and it wasn't the heat, at least not from the sun, that did it.

Nancy walked home, her cheeks flushed and warm. The cats clamored and mewed to be fed, and she dumped Fancy Feast into their bowls before heading upstairs to take a shower. It was when she was standing nude before the full-length mirror on the back of the door, that she noticed the clear imprint of a lipstick kiss on her cheek and it made her blush.

She stood there looking at her body in the mirror, the same body that had expelled six of their babies in the space of three years, all before she was four months pregnant, the same body Neil had come to loathe, protesting he was having sex with a "baby making machine." He said he felt "used" for his sperm, claimed she only wanted to have sex on schedule, when she was ovulating.

It wasn't true of course, not entirely. And she'd loved him without reserve. But even she had to admit, she'd gotten a little obsessive about the baby-making. Losing that much life in such a short span had done something to her. Some part of her had died with each miscarriage. Some plants you could prune, and they would come back stronger. Like roses. Some plants, like lilacs, were more delicate. If you pruned them, they didn't flower again for a very long time.

Nancy stood in front of the mirror, she didn't know how long, contemplating the lipstick mark and Gina's quip about switching teams, thinking about the hows and whys and whens of buds turning to blossoms.

* * * *

Nancy had started the party out in the cabana, and that's where she was ending it.

Her own swimsuit was an old, faded one-piece affair, nothing to write home about, but she'd forgotten one of the straps had broken on their last trip to Florida—she mended it with a safety pin—and there was a hole on the right side along the seam, where she'd caught it on the edge of a slide in the water park.

Neil had loved that park, running to the top of the slide with his tube again and again like a little kid, and all Nancy could think was how great it would be if they actually had their own little kid, even one of the lost six would have been a blessing and a miracle. But that was over, and she didn't have time to buy a new suit, and when she told her neighbor she didn't think she could come and the reason why, well somehow she had ended up in the cabana, changing into one of Gina's.

It had taken her neighbor half an hour to convince Nancy to come out after she changed. Outside, Gina had picked the perfect day for a pool party, the weather in full cooperation, the sun sinking low over the horizon as dusk approached but the air still plenty warm enough to go swimming.

"Come on," Gina begged from the other side of the door. "You can't stay in there all night!"

The party was already underway by then, and Nancy had entertained that very thought—she could just stay in the cabana. All night. There was plenty of room to recline on the padded bench, and she could just curl up and take a nap until everyone went home. But it was all Gina's relentless cajoling and begging and pleading that finally wore her down, and Nancy found the courage to open the door, stepping out of the cabana in a shockingly red bikini.

Gina's eyes widened. "Damn! What were you being so shy about? You rock that suit, girl! Let's get you a drink!"

Nancy didn't drink, but she decided it was a very good idea. Gina had hired a DJ and a bartender, and her friends were taking advantage of both, dancing and drinking and, of course, swimming. Nancy thought she'd never seen so much flesh in her life. She gulped down her first drink, something tangy and fruity and it burned all the way down her throat to her belly, then asked the bartender for another.

Gina started introducing her to people, telling them all about her neighbor with the green thumb and her amazing medicinal garden.

"I've been using this rose-oil stuff on my eyes. Carly, look at this!" Gina blinked at a bleached blonde with roots desperately in need of touching up and a stunningly contrasting tan. "Gone! It's like magic! You should buy some from Nancy!"

Nancy looked between them, blinking. "Oh, um… it's…"

"Rose oil," Gina said, putting an arm around her neighbor's shoulder. "It's just forty dollars for one bottle!"

Nancy gaped at her, but Carly seemed very interested, as did her brunette friend, and before she knew it, Nancy had fifteen women who wanted to buy a bottle of her rose oil at forty dollars a pop. Gina had already made a list, taking orders at the bar, when a young, tall, dark-haired guy with a six-pack—not the beer-kind, the body-kind—came over to tell Gina something about someone throwing up in the house.

Gina sighed, leaning over to Nancy. "You stay here. I'll be right back."

Nancy wasn't about to go anywhere. She sat and just watched, gulping down another drink and ordering a third, wishing Gina would come back. And soon. The pool was a huge, rectangular affair, all lit up in the darkness, everyone splashing and laughing and shouting to each other. How many people were there? Fifty? A hundred?

"Let's play 'I've Never!'" Carly came up to the bar to order a round of shots. She was followed by a group of both women and men, who grabbed their shot glasses and tried to cajole a bottle of whiskey out of the bartender.

"We *need* it," Carly insisted. She was already slurring her words. "Otherwise we can't play the game!"

"I'll fill your shots right here," the bartender countered. He was older, probably fifty, salt-and-pepper hair, wearing a Jimmy Buffet Hawaiian shirt with a parrot on the back, but as laid back as he looked, he wasn't going to let them get away with anything.

"Fine!" Carly huffed, and the group gathered around, half a dozen of them, pulling up and sitting on bar stools, surrounding and trapping Nancy. "Let's see... I've never...had sex in a canoe."

Just one guy stood up and did his shot.

"Oh my god, Gary!" The blonde gaped at him. "You've had sex in a canoe?"

The curly-haired guy with glasses—Gary—flipped off the blonde and sat down. "I was a camp counselor at the YMCA for ten years."

The crowd laughed.

"You know what they say about American beer?" The bartender went down the line pouring shots. "It's like having sex in a canoe."

"Huh?" Gary cocked his head.

"It's fucking close to water." The bartender put a shot in front of Nancy, including her because she was sitting there, his little joke getting a good laugh.

"He's going to say something he's never done before." Carly leaned in to explain the game to Nancy. "You have to stand up and take a shot if you've done it."

"Okay," Nancy agreed faintly. If the statements were anything like what had already been mentioned, it wasn't likely she would ever have to take a drink, but unfortunately, she couldn't slip away. She was surrounded. She glanced over to where Gina had disappeared into the house, willing her to come back out.

The brunette in the white biking sitting between Carly and Nancy—she thought her name was Sarah—stood up and said, "I've never... had sex in a confessional."

"Gary!" Carly exclaimed as he stood and took another shot. No one else did. "Again?"

He grinned. "Catholic school."

"Your turn," Carly said, nudging Nancy, who stood very reluctantly.

"I've never..." She swallowed, looking around at all the eyes on her. What in the world could she say? *I've never had a baby. I've never been with someone who really loves me no matter what. I've never told anyone how lonely I am.* "I've never... gone skinny dipping."

The group goggled at her like she had said something so shocking they couldn't quite believe it. Carly giggled, her eyes like blue sparks as she downed her shot. Every other person holding a shot glass did the same.

"Skinny dipping!" Carly called, taking off her bikini top and waving it over her head. "Time for skinny dipping!"

The guys hooted and cat-called, and before Nancy could blink, everyone around the bar was peeling off their suits and jumping in the pool. Nancy looked at the bartender, wide-eyed.

"First time at one of Gina's parties?" he inquired with a grin.

Nancy watched with growing horror as the trend caught on. People abandoned their bathing suits left and right, leaving them beside the pool and jumping into the water. Before long, she found herself the only one wearing any clothes at all, with the exception of the bartender and the DJ; all of the guests were naked and pairing up in the water.

"Excuse me," Nancy said faintly, not looking at the bartender but hearing him chuckle.

She thought about going home, but didn't want to abandon Gina's party without saying goodbye. She thought about going into the house to look for her neighbor, but didn't want to bother her if she was dealing with something serious or important. So instead, Nancy slipped quietly into the cabana again, the same place she'd started out the night and that's where she was dozing when Gina slipped inside.

"Well here you are."

Nancy half-sat, still dazed from sleep. "I'm sorry. I just…"

"I should have told you." Gina sat beside her on the long, padded bench. The top of the cabana was canvas, attached higher than the paneled cedar walls, letting in both light and sound. The party was still going on, but it was more subdued. "Everyone knows clothing is optional at my pool parties."

"I should go home." Nancy stood, but Gina stopped her, taking her wrist and tugging her slowly away from the door.

"You don't want to go out there."

Nancy swallowed, looking down at where Gina was circling her wrist with her hand. Her touch was so hot it almost burned. "Why not?"

"Everyone's having sex." Gina smirked. "Poor Mr. Desoto. He's going to have a stroke."

"Oh." She blinked, relenting to Gina's gentle tug and sitting beside her on the bench. Their thighs were touching, and the incredible softness of her neighbor's skin was a surprise to her system, making her breath come a little faster.

"I'm sorry if you're shocked." Gina leaned in a little, pressing her shoulder into Nancy's, nudging her.

"Oh... no. I'm not. Not really," Nancy protested, but the smirk on Gina's face just grew, her eyebrows rising with every denial.

"Really?" Gina stood, taking her neighbor's hand and heading for the door. "You want to join in then?"

"No, no!" Nancy shook her head furiously, pulling on Gina's hand, desperate.

"No..." Gina smiled, coming to stand in front of her neighbor, and Nancy found herself face-to-face with her perfectly shaped navel. She gazed up, up, up, past the swell of Gina's breasts in her white bikini top, meeting her neighbor's twinkling eyes. "Maybe we should start in here first?"

"Start?" Nancy squeaked, swallowing as Gina sank slowly to her knees, making them eye-level now, so close she could smell the alcohol on her breath, something light and fruity. Nancy could still taste her last drink, and she was feeling that light, floaty feeling she got whenever she drank, which wasn't often.

"Tell me if you want me to stop," Gina breathed before bridging the gap between them with a kiss. Her mouth was soft and open, her lips like velvet, Gina's hands on either side of the bench, not touching her, just kissing. Nancy realized about halfway through it was the most delightful thing that had ever happened to her as Gina's tongue found its way between her lips, exploring.

Nancy just blinked when they parted, unable to say a word. Taking her silence as consent, Gina bridged the gap again, kissing her, this time putting her hands on Nancy's hips, her fingers dancing along the curve of her waist, and then, oh then, cupping her breasts. Gina's thumbs grazed her nipples through the red material of her borrowed bikini, and Nancy moaned into her neighbor's mouth.

"Doesn't that feel good?" Gina breathed as they parted, her thumbs still rubbing, back and forth. Nancy just moaned again, looking at her through half-closed eyes. It had been so long, too long, since anyone had touched her—even just a casual hug or a kiss on the cheek—that her senses were overloaded with the attention.

"You'll tell me if you want me to stop?"

"Yes," Nancy breathed as Gina's lips tickled her neck, her shoulder, her fingers untying the bikini top fastened behind her neck. "Oh yes, I… ohhh!"

Gina's mouth moved to Nancy's nipple. Her breasts were average size, her nipples dark and very large, filling almost all of her areola, and they were incredibly sensitive. She moaned and arched, her hands moving in the mass of Gina's red hair, pulling her even closer as her neighbor continued to suckle her. The hot sensation of Gina's mouth engulfing her, the wet tongue flicking back and forth, teasing her nipple, made Nancy's toes curl with pleasure. And just when she thought she couldn't stand it for another moment, Gina moved to the other one.

But that didn't mean she abandoned the first. Gina stroked the wet nipple she had deserted with her fingertips as she suckled at the other, and Nancy felt herself parting her thighs, welcoming the pressing weight of Gina's breasts against her belly, as if she could simply absorb her through her flesh. Nancy glanced down, meeting Gina's eyes—she was watching her, listening, paying close attention to her response—and suddenly found it so strange she had to stop.

"Wait, no…" Nancy gasped, twisting away. She had an urge to run, or at least to hide her face. "I have to go!"

She bolted, forgetting she was half undressed only when she pulled the door open, but the sight that awaited her left her paralyzed, frozen in place, eyes growing wide with every passing second. When Gina had said everyone was having sex, she clearly hadn't been kidding. Everywhere she looked, there were naked people kissing, touching, licking, sucking, even fucking. It was a banquet of skin, a mass of flesh, and anyone who wasn't participating—there were a few, here and there, she noted—seemed to bat an eyelash.

Nancy felt Gina's arms go around her waist, the press of her neighbor's ample breasts pressed against her back, her breath hot against her ear, lips moving over her neck. Nancy didn't stop her. The fear she'd felt a moment ago began to melt as she watched the blonde—Carly, she remembered—on her knees on a towel in front of six-pack, sucking his cock deep into her throat. It was a stunning and fascinating sight.

"You're so beautiful, Nancy," Gina whispered into her ear, one hand moving up to cup Nancy's breast, the other heading south, cupping her mound. Nancy gasped and closed her eyes, leaning her head back against Gina's shoulder. The woman clearly had skills, her fingers moving over Nancy's red borrowed bikini bottoms in such a way she thought she might climax right there.

"I want you so much," Gina urged, hand moving faster, thumbing her nipple. "I've wanted you since the first time I saw you out front, pruning your rose bushes in those sexy little cut-offs…"

Her words made Nancy blush, but her body was responding. She couldn't help herself. She whimpered, rocking against Gina, their hips moving together as they watched the display of flesh in front of them.

"Let me touch you," Gina begged, her mouth raining kisses over her shoulder. "Let me make you feel good. Will you let me?"

"Yes," Nancy moaned, turning in her arms and pressing herself against her neighbor. She couldn't deny her body one moment more. "Oh yes, please. Yes."

Gina closed and locked the cabana door and they found their way to the padded bench, kissing and touching in the fading light. The darkness was a relief to Nancy as Gina stripped her down to nothing, exclaiming in delight over Nancy's body with such enthusiasm it made her blush. She was embarrassed by her own lust, by the way her body twisted and arched for more, but she couldn't help it.

"Just let go," Gina encouraged her, pressing Nancy onto her back and stretching her out naked on the bench. There was enough room for Gina to settle herself between her neighbor's thighs, and that's just what she did, kissing around the dark triangle of hair framing Nancy's sopping wet pussy. Nancy was so wet she was ashamed of it, feeling her juices running down the crack of her ass and pooling on the bench beneath her.

"Oh God, you smell so good," Gina moaned, nuzzling her cheek against the curly, soft hair of Nancy's pubes. "Can I taste you? Please?"

"Yes!" Nancy cried, lifting her hips in encouragement, knowing if someone had told her a month ago something like this might happen, she would have laughed, and not caring, not caring at all. She wanted this. More than anything. She'd been curious about it since she first saw Gina walking around nude in her backyard and had actively thought about it since she had spied on her neighbor masturbating.

Gina's tongue parted Nancy's fat, swollen pussy lips, working slowly back and forth, teasing. Nancy whimpered, shifting her hips, aching for relief. She couldn't believe how aroused she was, how right on the edge. Her level of excitement made her tremble and gasp under Gina's attention. The sweetness was too much, the way her body ached for more and yet never wanted it to end.

There was no holding back the flood of pleasure that made her thighs quiver with taut anticipation. She tried. She made a valiant effort, her hands tangling in Gina's hair, pushing her away, pulling her closer, hips rocking to and fro, but there was no escaping it. Her orgasm rocked both of them, Nancy's tremors forcing Gina to wrap her arms around her, keeping her mouth focused and centered right on her throbbing clit.

"Ohhh! Gina!" And then there were no words. Nancy let herself go completely in her neighbor's arms, coming and coming, flooding Gina's tongue in hot, pulsing waves. Her climax was so intense she had to throw her arm over her mouth to keep from screaming, biting her own flesh so hard she would have a bruise there for a week.

"Mmmm." Gina kissed Nancy's mound, soft and gentle and sweet, chuckling softly at the way Nancy gasped and trembled and whispered to herself as she floated back down to earth.

"Ohmygodohmygodohmyfuckinggod," she whispered over and over, still shivering.

Gina tickled Nancy's lower belly lightly with her nails, drawing a sensuous line down the center of her triangle to her slit, making Nancy shiver with post-orgasmic delight.

"Now..." Gina's finger parted Nancy's pussy lips, which felt fatter and more swollen, her clit still pulsing. "Let's see if we can do that again."

Nancy's eyes flew open wide as Gina spread her, flicking her tongue at the top of her cleft, forcing a shudder through her. Nancy protested, wiggling and writhing on the bench, moving her hips, trying to escape from the sweet torture of her neighbor's relentless tongue, but it was no use. Gina had her by the hips now, mouth fastened over her mound, the tenacious press of her tongue sending Nancy flying higher than she ever thought possible.

"Oh my God, what are you doing?" Nancy moaned, hips lifting, not sure if her body was trying to escape or if it was actually asking for more. Goosebumps rose over her flesh, her breath came faster and faster still, the excessive, overwhelming sensation transforming into something else, as if her clitoris was a little reset button and Gina had found just the way to press it.

And then they were off to the races again, Nancy rocking and spreading her thighs for the greedy lick and suck of Gina's hungry mouth, so lost in the feeling she forgot about everything, about the people just outside who might hear her moans, about the fact her neighbor was a woman, and she'd never been with a woman sexually, she hardly knew her, really, and yet here they were, locked together in a dance of pleasure Nancy hadn't known was even possible.

"Oh! Oh! I'm coming! Again! Oh fuck!" Nancy's hips shot upward, toes curling, hands grabbing onto Gina's wrists, shoving her pussy against her neighbor's mouth. Gina lapped and lapped, never letting up, taking Nancy's climax in and swallowing her, the soft nibble and suck of her lips coaxing more and more sweet spasms from Nancy's quivering flesh.

And then Gina was kissing her, the women embracing in the softest of kisses. Nancy could taste herself on Gina's tongue, smell her own pussy, and it excited her beyond belief. How had she never known she tasted so good? Neil had never liked to do *that*—although he would, on occasion, if she reciprocated. He used to make jokes about fish and tuna until she just stopped asking. But she'd never once tasted for herself.

"Do you like the way you taste?" Gina smiled down at her, the weight of her body a delight, all soft flesh and sinew, her full breasts pressed into Nancy's.

"Mmm." Nancy licked her lips. "Do *you* taste like that?"

She never thought she would ask such a question, but she couldn't help remembering watching Gina touch herself, how the woman's fiery bush had blazed in the sunlight, and how the lips below had been smooth and bare. What was that like, she wondered?

Gina smirked. "Similar, I imagine."

"Let me make you feel good too," Nancy breathed, daring to reach her hand down and cup her neighbor's mound. Her suit was still fully on, but the crotch of her bikini was hot and damp.

"Are you sure?" Gina hesitated, but Nancy was nodding, a little shy but eager too. Her hand was already moving between Gina's thighs, making the redhead moan with pleasure. Nancy didn't realize what an incredible incentive that would be, hearing her lust.

"I'm not sure what I'm doing..." Nancy confessed as Gina stood, untying her suit, sliding off her bottoms. Seeing her nude was common enough now, but somehow this was different. Her body seemed suddenly more abundant, full of cracks and crevices Nancy was unsure of.

Gina smiled, stretching out on the bench and letting her knees fall open. "Just do what you know feels good for you."

Nancy crawled between her neighbor's spread thighs, marveling as she touched them, how soft and smooth she was. Remembering what Gina had done, she kissed her way upward, avoiding the already-glistening and swollen mound between her thighs, tracing a line up to her navel with her lips. There was a piercing there and Nancy flicked it with her tongue, feeling Gina shiver with anticipation.

And then she reached the twin mountains of her breasts, pink-tipped, the nipples very hard. When she took the first one into her mouth, Gina gasped, her eyelids fluttering closed. Nancy sucked and licked gently, practicing there with her tongue, pretending for a moment it was a clit, remembering just what Gina had done to her.

"That's it," Gina urged, and Nancy felt her hips moving in slow circles beneath her. "Lick it just like that."

She abandoned that nipple and switched to the other, bathing it with her tongue. The more she wet it, the more Gina seemed to like it, so she didn't even bother swallowing all her saliva, letting it flood her nipple.

"Oh God, my pussy's on fire," Gina whimpered, hips rocking. "Please. Please!"

Nancy let Gina guide her, pressing her down, down, down between her legs. She could smell her, the same musky scent, and the first time she pressed her lips to Gina's cleft and tasted her, she tasted herself too, the sweet tang. It was heady, delightful, and she dove in for more.

"Oh!" Gina cried out in surprise as Nancy sucked and nibbled at her clit. Gina's lips were soft and smooth, her only pubic hair at the top of her cleft. It tickled Nancy's nose.

"Is it okay?" Nancy paused, licking the taste off her lips, feeling Gina's juices on her chin.

"Yes!" Gina nodded, biting her lip as she looked down between her legs. Her fingers were working her own nipples, rubbing and tugging. "Oh yes! Keep licking!"

Nancy did, working her tongue back and forth over the little button of her clitoris. The sound of Gina's moans, the way her hips rolled, made her lick faster, press harder. She wanted to give her as much pleasure as possible.

"Put your fingers in me," Gina gasped, spreading wider. "Please! Finger-fuck me!"

Nancy did as she was asked, sliding one finger inside, but that wasn't enough, because Gina begged for more, more, until she had three fingers pumping in and out of her flesh, fucking her with such force, Gina's moans were punctuated with a jarring gasp at each thrust.

"Fuck! Fuck! Fuck!" Gina cried out, hips lifting, her whole body trembling. "Ooooohhh I'm coming! Nowwwww!"

Nancy didn't know what to do, so she just kept doing what she'd been doing, flicking her tongue over Gina's quivering clit, driving her fingers harder and faster into her pussy, surprised at the snap and flutter of Gina's muscles as her climax rattled through her. Gina's cries grew softer, her body slowly relaxing, and Nancy slowed too, her tongue barely moving, her fingers still.

"Holy fuck." Gina took a deep, shuddering breath. "You made me come so hard my ears are ringing."

Nancy flooded with delight at her words. She was strangely proud of herself.

"Come here." Gina pulled Nancy to her and the women kissed. Nancy giggled when Gina started licking her lips and chin, cleaning her off, like a cat. She rested her cheek on Gina's breast, tucking her head under her chin, and they stayed that way a while. Outside, the music was still playing, and from the sound of it, people were still partying. So to speak.

"You know, I usually have a pool party once a month or so..." Gina murmured, kissing the top of Nancy's head. "And you have a standing invitation."

"Do I have to wait that long?" Nancy lifted her face, looking at Gina in the dimness, surprised by her own boldness. There was very little light coming in now, but she could see the outline of her expression, the softness in her face.

Gina kissed her. "No. Definitely not."

They snuggled again, breathing slow and even now, and Nancy found she couldn't stop smiling. She thought Gina might be sleeping, and she might have even slept herself, her thoughts drifting.

"Queen of the Andes..." Nancy murmured happily.

"Hmm?"

"There's a plant in Bolivia that flowers just once in its lifetime," Nancy explained softly. "She lives eighty to a hundred years long, and she flowers just once, right before she dies."

"That's the Queen of the Andes?" Gina asked.

"Uh-huh. There are some flowers that bloom every year," Nancy went on, lifting her face and looking at her neighbor, tracing the line of Gina's jaw with her finger. "There are even some, like you, that bloom year round. And there are some that bloom just once. Like me."

Gina shook her head, wrapping her arms around Nancy's shoulders and kissing the top of her head. "I think you got it wrong. I think you're a sweet, soft, delicate rosebud. You just needed all the right conditions to bloom."

Nancy considered this, smiling in the darkness. "Mmm. And now that I've found those perfect conditions...?"

"Roses come back, don't they?" Gina asked.

Nancy nodded. "They do."

"Well, I think you'll be coming back again... and again..." Gina kissed her and they rolled and giggled together in the darkness, and Nancy knew she was absolutely right.

First Time

Molly hated fast food—couldn't stand the sight or smell of it, in any way, shape, or form. Most of her girlfriends claimed they hated it too, but they ate it—Chicken McNuggets and fries, double bacon cheeseburgers, all with Diet Cokes, of course. Molly truly couldn't. It made her gag just to walk by a McDonalds. She had some weird food aversions, it was true. She hated both shrimp (the eyes and veins!) and broccoli—like eating little trees. Blah. But fast food was the worst. She'd seen one picture of the "pink slime" they make nuggets out of and was done.

That was honestly why she started babysitting. Her friends all had seven-dollar-an-hour jobs working the drive-thru, handing out hot coffee and sausage biscuits and hash browns before school, but Molly couldn't walk into a McDonalds let alone get a job there. So she was stuck finding babysitting jobs, getting paid anywhere from five to ten dollars an hour, depending on the family. It wasn't a steady paycheck and it left a lot to be desired at the end of the month when she wanted to splurge on an outfit or a concert.

That was why finding Faith was such a godsend.

They met through an ad Faith put on Craigslist.

Cool single mom, loves her baby boy, but also loves to go out and party and have fun. Who says you can't have it all? Need a reliable babysitter for weekend nights, Friday and Saturday for sure, some weeknights, depending on my work schedule, someone responsible who loves babies (he's nine months, sleeps through the night, it's an easy job!)

Molly had responded without a lot of hope. She was still in high school, just turned eighteen in January, and while most of her families had been hiring her for years and she had great references, she had a feeling the cool single mom, in spite of her partying ways, had pretty high standards. She was probably looking for Mary Poppins or Supernanny. She even considered putting on a suit and an accent but knew it wouldn't fool anyone, so she went in her jeans and her geeky Dr. Who t-shirt with not a lot of expectations or hope.

It turned out it was the best thing she could have done.

"Oh my God, I love *Dr. Who!*" That was the first thing out of Faith's mouth when she opened her apartment door for the interview. "Seriously, I'm totally on a Netflix marathon."

"Awesome!" Molly laughed, looking at the baby on the woman's hip. He was a big, blond boy with wide, dark eyes. He looked a lot like his Mom. Even the round cheeks and curls around his face and little rosebud mouth. "Cute baby."

"This is Gilmore."

"Gilmore? As in Happy?"

"Isn't he?" Faith laughed, swinging the door wider and inviting her in. "I had a weird thing for Adam Sandler when he was born. Besides, his father wanted to name him Huffington Post and call him HuffPo for short, so it was the better of the two, as far as I was concerned."

"Well it's better than North West," Molly agreed. "Where is his dad?"

They settled in like two girls having a casual conversation around the kitchen table while the baby—Gil—crawled happily around on the tile floor with a sippy cup and a Cheerios bowl, occasionally banging against their legs for attention and getting it. Molly was amazed how easy it was to talk to Faith, but she was still pretty young—just twenty-eight—and they liked all the same things.

Except that Faith, unlike Molly, loved to go out dancing. That was the one thing they didn't have in common. Dr Who? Check. Tosh.O? Check. IFunny? Check. But dancing? Molly didn't do that. Besides, she spent her weekends and free time babysitting, not going out to the clubs with her friends. And most of her friends were out dancing and teen clubbing and having a great night life—those that weren't already hooked up with some steady guy, that is. Those girls were usually out on dates at the movies, or holed up in some unsuspecting parents' basement having sex on leather couches.

Molly hadn't ever done any of those things. She was still a virgin and thought she'd probably stay that way a long time, if the boys at school were any indication of what was available out there. Unless August "Gus" Coleman happened to glance her way one day and suddenly find her utterly irresistible. But that was about as likely as hell freezing over in July.

That's what she thought, until today.

Her literal run-in with Gus Coleman as she ran to catch the bus had her so flustered, she forgot to give Gil his bottle before bed and he woke up crying and hungry at midnight. She fed the baby his formula while he suckled like a greedy little piglet and she daydreamed about that afternoon.

Not only had Gus Coleman apologized for his clumsiness—while it had been her usual head-down, headlong pace that actually caused the altercation—he had picked up her books and when she glanced up to meet his eyes, he'd asked her name—never mind they'd gone to school together since they were in kindergarten—her name tripped off her tongue and when he repeated it with a bemused smile on his face, she thought she just might faint right there on the spot.

She'd gone out at lunch with her friend, Mandy—Mandy's parents were rich and had given her a car for her sixteenth birthday—and was still carrying around her Slurpee as she ran for the bus. Mandy usually drove her home, but she had track practice after school. Which was why many of Molly's textbooks were now splattered with red frozen slush.

"Aw, man, let me get you a new one." Gus tucked her AP English book—*A Farewell to Arms*—onto the stack she was carrying. "I go right by 7-11 on my way home. Cherry?"

"Uhhh... I have to go." She had just blinked at him, wondering how in the hell he knew she was a virgin, before she realized he was just guessing her Slurpee flavor.

Molly had rushed onto the bus, finding a seat near the back and crouching down low. He didn't pursue her and while part of her was grateful, another part of her realized she'd just let maybe the biggest opportunity of her life pass her by. She watched, feeling sick to her stomach, as Gus Coleman's red Mustang GT rolled by, purring like a cat.

Gus Coleman had offered her a ride home—*and she had refused.*

She put a milk-sleepy Gil back in his crib, still lamenting this fact as she curled up on the couch in front of a re-run of *Friends* and imagined it all happening differently. What if she'd said yes, instead of running off like a scared rabbit? What if she'd laughed and did that hair-flip thing all the popular girls had perfected—although with her short, bobbed dark hair and glasses, it probably wouldn't have come across the same way. Her glasses would have flown off and landed under the bus or something, with her luck.

Even in her imagination, she couldn't be sexy!

By the time Faith was sticking her key into the deadbolt, Molly was fast asleep. She heard the key but was in the middle of an incredible dream about Gus Coleman. Her conscious mind couldn't seem to go there, but her unconscious had no problems, apparently, stripping her naked in front of the only boy she'd had a crush on since their first day of kindergarten. Not only were they naked, but they were kissing and touching and rubbing and oh my God, it all felt so good she thought she might explode with pleasure...

And then Faith was shaking her gently awake and the image of Gus and his lean, hard body slowly faded to black. Molly could smell the alcohol on Faith's breath and she opened her eyes to see the older woman's smiling face, her blond hair a mass of curls, eyes dark and soft, like a doe's.

"Morning, sleepyhead," Faith slurred, a motherly hand stroking the back of Molly's cheek. "Some dream?"

"Huh?" Molly half-sat, flushing a bright, hot red.

"You were moaning and called out... some guy's name... Gus?"

Molly thought she couldn't turn any redder and Faith laughed at her response, tossing her purse onto the sofa and standing to slip off her heels. Faith's club attire was always flashy, short and revealing. Her little white and silver slip dress was no exception. It rode high up on her thighs, high enough for Molly to wonder if she was wearing underwear as she bent to undo the straps on her strappy silver heels.

"So spill!" Faith curled up on the other end of the sofa, her long legs folded under her. "Who's Gus?"

"No one." Molly shook her head vehemently, knowing her answer only made it more obvious.

"Did he ask you out?" Faith asked, leaning forward eagerly. "Is he cute?"

"No." Molly sat, cross-legged in her jeans and t-shirt, on the couch facing Faith. "Well, he kind of asked me to go somewhere with him but I... didn't. And yes... he's a hottie."

Faith squealed, sounding delighted. "So why didn't you go out with him?"

"I don't know." Molly pushed her glasses up on her nose. It was the question she'd been asking herself all night. "Because... I guess... I don't know, Faith. I'm not like you."

"What do you mean by that?" Faith raised her fair, delicately arched eyebrows with a smirk.

"Nothing bad." Molly flushed. "I'm just not, you know, used to flirting with guys and being..."

"A slut?" Faith's eyebrows rose further.

"I didn't say that!" The heat in Molly's cheeks was unbearable.

"You know, just because a woman likes sex, that doesn't make her a slut." Faith leaned over and tucked

Molly's short, dark hair behind her ears. "There shouldn't be any shame in sex, ever. For any gender."

"Do you?" Molly licked her lips, surprised at her own daring. "Like sex, I mean?"

"Of course." Faith laughed, throwing her arms wide and leaning back on the couch. She was drunker than usual tonight. "Sex feels good. What's not to like?"

"It's all..." Molly sighed, crossing her arms and sitting back on the couch. "It's all so complicated. I mean, I like boys. I think about them. You know, kissing and touching and... things."

"Things?" Faith snorted, leaning her elbow on the back of the couch, her chin in hand. "Have you ever even kissed a boy?"

Molly shook her head miserably, meeting the older girl's eyes.

"Poor girl." Faith commiserated. "It all seems complicated, but it's really very simple."

"No it isn't." Molly laughed, shaking her head, hair flying. She wished she could hide. Disappear completely. Be invisible. Faith said it wasn't complicated, that there shouldn't be any shame in it, but she couldn't see how. It all felt overwhelming, impossible. The mechanics alone, of what went where, when and how, were enough to make her break out into a cold sweat.

"Want me to show you?" Faith slid closer to her on the sofa, winding a soft, slender arm around her neck. "Then when he kisses you, you'll know what to do."

"Show... me?" Molly's breath stopped and so did her heart as she looked into the woman's beautiful doe eyes. She was so pretty it was almost hard to look at her fully—like looking at the sun. Faith couldn't possibly mean what it sounded like?

"Like this." Faith leaned in so close Molly had to close her eyes and when she did, Faith's lips touched hers.

It was a light, feathery kiss, a sort of asking—*Okay? More? Yes?* Faith's hand moved over her shoulder, pulling her closer, and Molly gasped as their upper bodies pressed together, Faith's full breasts mashing against her smaller, pert ones. Her gasp gave Faith an opening and she took it, tongue snaking out to lick Molly's lips, dancing so delightfully in her mouth, she felt it all the way to her toes.

When they parted, Molly sat, mouth half-open, eyes dazed, brain full and throbbing with the experience. And that wasn't all that was full and throbbing. The kiss had ignited a spark between her legs that licked at her thighs with heat. She was on fire—everything burned.

"Did you like it?" Faith breathed. She smelled and tasted like alcohol, something sweet and fruity.

Molly nodded slowly, unable to deny it.

"Want me to do it again?"

Molly nodded again, biting her lip. She did want her to do it again. She wanted it very much.

Faith tilted Molly's chin up, eyes searching for the truth. She seemed satisfied with what she saw because she leaned in to capture Molly's mouth again, her lips impossibly soft, her tongue like pink velvet. It was a strange and wonderful sensation, something Molly had thought about and dreamed of—of course, she'd been thinking about doing this with a boy, not another woman.

"Is this wrong?" Molly gasped when they parted. Faith's hands circled her waist, pulling her closer with a little smile.

"Does it feel wrong?" she whispered, feathering kisses on Molly's neck, making her shiver.

Molly didn't know how to answer that question. Her body certainly didn't think it was wrong—her nipples hardened like pebbles under her t-shirt, aching to be touched, and the heat between her legs was like an inferno—but her brain was giving her all sorts of mixed messages. She liked Faith, thought she was very pretty, had admired her for a long time. But was she attracted to her? Did she like girls? Did this mean—

"I'm not a lesbian," Molly insisted as Faith's hands moved slowly up her waist.

"Neither am I." Faith nuzzled her, running her tongue along Molly's collarbone. "I'm just showing you how it works."

"But..." Molly moaned softly when Faith's hands moved up to cup the girl's little breasts in her hands, her thumbs moving back and forth over her hard nipples. "It's not the same. I mean... as it would be, with a boy."

"Not exactly." Faith smiled, her gaze dipping down to Molly's chest where she continued petting her nipples through her shirt. It made Molly feel weak-kneed and dizzy. "But if you'll let me show you, I bet you'll be a lot more relaxed with... what was his name again?"

"Gus?" Molly whispered faintly as Faith pulled her t-shirt up, exposing her bra. She'd almost forgotten about him. Would he kiss her like this? Touch her this way?

"Your nipples are sensitive aren't they?" Faith undid Molly's front-hook bra with one expert motion. Molly had never been naked in front of anyone before, unless you counted her mother, and that was back when she was eight. She felt shy and moved to cover herself, but Faith caught her wrists in her hands.

"Don't." Faith's gaze skipped up from her breasts to her face, shaking her blonde head. "You're so beautiful."

"Me?" Molly blinked in surprise at her words, at the unmistakable look of lust in Faith's eyes. She'd never felt beautiful in her whole life, but the way Faith looked at her made her feel that way.

"Come here." Faith held out her hand and Molly took it, following the older girl down the hallway, past the baby's room, into Faith's bedroom. She had a big queen sized bed which took up most of it. Faith sat her on the bed, reaching down to pull off Molly's t-shirt and bra. Molly let her and didn't even cover herself as she watched Faith slip her little white dress over her head, answering the question about whether she was wearing a bra or panties underneath.

She was wearing neither.

Molly stared in awe and wonder at her body—full breasts with big, pink nipples, her mound shaved completely except for a strip of curly blond fuzz at the top. Her hips were full, her navel pierced, and she had a tattoo on her side of a colorful hummingbird whose bill pointed upward, like he wanted to draw nectar from her breast.

"Are you scared?" Faith asked, touching her cheek.

Molly shook her head. She wasn't afraid, not exactly. Excited, yes. Anticipant. Nervous, maybe. But not afraid.

"Good." Faith sat beside her on the bed, sliding her arm around Molly's waist. She was nude from the waist up now and the touch of Faith's bare skin was dizzying as they kissed again. She was getting used to the sensation of kissing, the delicious feel of their tongues meshing, but when Faith pulled her fully into her arms, their bare breasts flattening against one another, Molly couldn't help the moan that escaped her throat.

They leaned back together on the bed, like collapsing onto the softest cloud, mouths moving, hands too. Molly didn't know where to put hers, but she couldn't help touching the softness of Faith's skin, petting her shoulder, her side where the hummingbird forever strained to reach the older girl's breast. Faith, however, didn't have any inhibitions. She ran her hands over Molly's body, her fingers teasing the girl's bare nipples, a sensation that sent such delicious sensations directly between Molly's thighs, she thought they were like little "on" buttons.

Molly had done a little experimenting with her own body—touching her nipples through her nightgown, twisting in the sheets at night, her hand tucked between her legs, rubbing, rubbing, rubbing, never getting any relief—but she'd never felt anything like the sensation of Faith's mouth fastened over her hard, dark nipple. It made her hand move between her own legs, cupping her mound through her jeans, feeling the incredible heat there.

"That's right," Faith instructed, reaching down, unbuttoning and unzipping Molly's jeans. "Do what feels good."

"Don't stop doing that," Molly gasped, wiggling out of her jeans. She left her panties on, some semblance of modesty, although she wasn't sure why.

"What? Licking them?" Faith smiled and flicked her tongue across the tip of her nipple. "Sucking them?"

Molly moaned when Faith's mouth covered her nipple again, fingers playing with the other, making Molly's hand move faster and faster between her legs. She had never understood this feeling, this wanting something more, always. She had often rubbed the wiry dark hair covering her labia until she felt raw and on the verge of something entirely new, but to no avail. There was never anything but breathless aching over every crest.

Faith spent a long, long time kissing and licking her nipples, first one, then the other, whispering often how beautiful Molly was, how lovely, how perfect. It made Molly glow from the inside out, the fire between her legs so intense she could barely breathe. When Faith began kissing her way down Molly's belly, she forgot how to breathe, and when her lips and tongue started tracing the elastic outline of Molly's panties, she didn't care if she ever breathed again.

"Have you ever made yourself come?" Faith wondered aloud, hooking her thumbs in Molly's panties and sliding them down her thighs.

"I... don't..." Molly shook her head, watching in wonder as the older girl kissed and nibbled and licked at her dark fuzz. Molly wasn't just hot down there, she was moist too. Wet and squishy and full to bursting.

"So this really is your first time." Faith brightened, slowly parting Molly's labia, easing her way into the flesh, exploring with her tongue. Molly stared in disbelief, up on her elbows. She'd heard about this—a few of her girlfriends at sleepovers had giggled and whispered and talked about oral sex, both giving and receiving—but she'd never understood. Not until the moment Faith's tongue found that spot, that throbbing, aching, sensitive spot, did she understand all the fuss.

But she understood now.

"Ohhh my God!" Molly moaned, head going back, knees falling apart, back arching in complete surrender to the lash of the older girl's persistent, velvet tongue. Faith moaned too but it was muffled because her mouth was fastened over Molly's swollen mound. It made her thighs tremble and her ass clench.

"Do you want to feel what a cock would be like?" Faith murmured, kissing that spot, the brush of her lips making Molly quiver. She didn't wait for an answer before sliding a finger inside, making Molly's body jolt in surprise. Then she slid two fingers in and Molly groaned at the sensation of being filled.

"One more," Faith urged, stretching Molly to the max, making her cry out as three fingers slid inside of her. "There. That's what a boy's cock would feel like sliding inside of you."

"Oh God." Molly bit her lip, eyes half-closed as she looked down at Faith slowly sliding her fingers in, then out, the soft squelch of her wetness filling the room. "Ohhhh yes!"

"You like that?" Faith smiled, nuzzling her mound with her nose. "Try this."

Faith's mouth found her again, sucking and licking and tasting and swallowing. Molly shuddered and bucked and thrust, more, *more*. Her mind raced. She couldn't focus. Her brain had forsaken her altogether and she became pure sensation. The fire between her legs was like a fever that wouldn't break. She was miserable, aching, shivering all over.

When it came—when *she* came—it was sudden and surprised her so much she cried out and backpedalled on the bed, her sex throbbing with release, finally, finally, such blessed, sweet relief. Molly stared, panting, open-mouthed, as Faith smiled slyly, her face glistening with Molly's juices.

"What... was... that?" Molly gasped, hand covering her own mound, still unable to quite believe the sensation that had overtaken her.

"That, dear girl, was an orgasm." Faith gave a throaty laugh, climbing up beside her on the bed to take stunned Molly into her arms. Molly let her, still trembling in shock. "That's what you want to make sure you feel *every* time you're with a boy. If he doesn't make that happen with his cock, then you make him use his fingers and his tongue, like I just did."

"That's never happened before," Molly whispered, turning her flushed cheek to rest against Faith's breast, her glasses fogged and all askew. "Even when I touched myself... I didn't know..."

"See why sex is so much fun?" Faith laughed, petting her neck, her shoulder. "Once I started, I could never get enough."

"When did you start?" Molly wondered aloud.

"I was fourteen." She kissed Molly's cheek, her lips soft, sweet. "A girl like you, so unexperienced, these days? You're like a..."

"Weirdo." Molly snorted a laugh. "I know."

"I wasn't going to say that." Faith kissed the tip of her nose. "You're like a dream come true. A blank slate."

"Can I do that again?" Molly asked, hearing Faith's low chuckle. "I mean, it can happen more than once, right?"

"Girls can do it a lot," Faith agreed. "Way more than guys. I can come over and over again. Especially during oral."

"Oral." Molly said the word, letting it roll off her tongue. "I like oral."

"Me too," Faith replied with a laugh.

Molly looked up at her, thoughtful. She'd never believed, in her wildest dreams, that something like this might happen. With Faith. With anyone, ever! But now that it had, she was glad. Not only that it had happened, but that it had been Faith, beautiful, kind, generous Faith. She was like an older, more experienced sister. Only not related, which made this all okay. Or, at least more okay.

"God, you turned me on." Faith sighed, sliding a hand down over her breast, tweaking her nipple. "Do you mind if I make myself come?"

"No, I don't mind." Molly watched as Faith's hand slipped lower, trailing over the softness of her belly, heading between her thighs. "You can do it yourself?"

"You've never touched yourself?" Faith half-smiled, sighing deeply as her fingers parted her labia.

"Well, a little," Molly admitted, up on an elbow, watching Faith's hand move. Her mound was completely shaved, glistening wet.

"You have to rub your clit," Faith instructed, parting her labia to show her. "Right here, up top. This little button. You have one. Feel."

She took Molly's hand, guiding it between Faith's thighs. It was so very slippery, slick and hot, but Molly felt it under her fingers, just like a little button. Faith rubbed it back and forth, moaning softly.

"Touch your pussy," Faith urged. "Go ahead."

Molly bit her lip, but she did it, parting her labia, just like she'd seen Faith do, fingers exploring the soft, swollen flesh between her legs. Oh God, there it was—the place Faith's tongue had focused on, her mouth driving Molly wild with lust. It throbbed under her fingers as she watched Faith touch her own pussy.

"You can come again," Faith assured her. "Do whatever feels good. I like to make circles with these two fingers, like this."

Molly watched, fascinated, as Faith covered her clit with her fingers and rubbed them around and around, slowly at first, then faster. Molly mimicked her movements, gasping at the sudden jolt, like an electric shock, when her fingers found her own clit, then moaning as the sensation took off. It was like the slow take-off to flying, a sweet build-up.

"God you taste so good." Faith licked her lips, eyes half-closed. "I can still taste you in my mouth."

"It tastes good?" Molly blinked in surprise. The thought had never occurred to her but now it intrigued her.

"Kiss me." Faith tilted her face up and Molly lowered her lips to hers, tasting, a musky tang. "See?"

"Mmm." Molly brightened, her gaze following the movement of Faith's fingers. "Can I taste you?"

Faith stopped breathing, her eyes widening in surprise.

"Are you sure?"

Molly nodded shyly. She wanted to. Not only was she curious, but she remembered how good it felt to have Faith's tongue between her legs, so much better than her own fingers, even now. Faith had given her a gift, and she wanted to give her one too.

"Only if you're sure," Faith said as Molly took off her glasses and put them on the night stand.

"I'm sure." She said the words, but when she was settled between Faith's thighs, she wasn't so sure anymore. Molly kissed her thigh, watching Faith touch herself, wondering what she'd just gotten herself into. She didn't have any idea what she was doing, after all.

"You don't have to." Faith touched Molly's hair as the younger girl rested her cheek against one of her spread thighs. "I can get myself off like this."

"Just... lick?" Molly frowned, watching Faith spread her lips, showing her up close. She'd never seen her own sex this close up before and was amazed the soft, pink inside, the labyrinth of flesh, the sensitive button up top, and the wink of a dark, wet hole near the bottom.

"Right here," Faith urged, framing her clit between her fingers. "Just lick here until you get tired... or I say stop."

"Okay." It sounded easy enough.

Molly touched her tongue to Faith's clit, feeling her shiver in response. She lifted her gaze to meet the older girl's eyes, moving her tongue back and forth over that little button. It didn't taste bad—that same tangy musk she'd experienced when she kissed Faith. In fact, she kind of liked it. She remembered how it felt, having Faith's tongue between her thighs, her fingers slipping in and out, taking her higher and higher.

Faith moaned, rocking her hips up, and Molly licked her faster, latching her mouth over her mound. Her skin was incredibly soft, completely smooth, her labia swollen and slick. Molly slid her hands up over Faith's belly, coming to rest on the older girl's breasts. They filled her hands deliciously and Faith moaned louder when Molly squeezed her nipples, rolling them between thumb and forefinger.

Molly's own pussy throbbed and she squeezed her legs together and tried to focus on Faith's pleasure. But it wasn't easy. The more Faith responded, the more exciting it became, the more her own sex ached for attention. She twisted her hips on the bed, lashing her tongue over Faith's clit again and again, hearing her breath coming faster, filling the room.

"Let me lick you," Faith moaned, reaching for her.

Molly shook her head—she wanted to make her come, wanting to give that to her—refusing to unfasten her mouth from Faith's swollen, slick mound.

"Yes! Come here!" Faith twisted around, turning, grabbing Molly's slim hips and yanking them so she was on top of the older girl. Molly could still reach Faith's pussy and re-fastened her mouth over her clit, licking and sucking furiously at her flesh, moaning all the while.

But her moans grew louder when Faith did the same to her, spreading Molly's labia so she could bury her face between her legs. Her aching pussy was finally getting the attention she'd craved, but it made it so damned hard to concentrate! She tried to stay focused, working her tongue around and around, the way Faith had done—was doing—to her, tracing the same path Faith had made with her fingers, but Faith's mouth made it almost impossible.

"Oh God!" Molly cried out. That sensation—taking off, leveling out, rising again, and then... then... "Oh God! Ohhhhh!"

Faith wrapped her arms around Molly's hips, her own bucking up against Molly's flickering tongue. There was no stopping it. Molly thrashed in her arms, her orgasm rising to a fever pitch, taking her with it as it crested and rolled through her. Nothing had ever felt this good in the universe, before or since, she was sure of it. Faith moaned against her sex and Molly felt her shudder and buck, her pussy spasming around Molly's exploring, probing fingers. She was coming, under her, all over her face, Faith was coming too.

"Oh sweetheart." Faith moaned softly, kissing the insides of Molly's trembling thighs. "You made me come so hard."

Molly turned, letting Faith pull her into her arms, their kiss blending the taste of their juices, a delicious, heady concoction. She thought she'd never taste anything so sweet in her life again. Faith breathed her in, pulling the comforter over them both. It was chilly now, their bodies shiny with sweat and more.

"Thank you," Molly said softly, snuggling against the rise of Faith's ample breasts. "For showing me."

"Mmmm, thank you for letting me." Faith kissed the top of her head. "Now when Gus goes to kiss you, you'll know what to do."

"Now I'll know just where to tell him I want to be kissed." Molly smiled, closing her eyes, feeling Faith's low laugh. "And how... and how often..."

"Good girl," Faith replied. "But you know... there's more I have to teach you."

"There is?" Molly's head came up in surprise, her body responding instantly with heat.

Faith nodded, grinning. "Lots more."

"I can't wait." Molly kissed her, full on the mouth, not even a little bit shy anymore.

"Me either," Faith murmured against Molly's lips as they lost themselves together once more.

It wasn't the first time—it could never be the first time again, Molly knew. But it wouldn't be the last time, either, and that made Molly happy.

Happier than she ever could say.

College Days

Whitney's Honey Longboard clacked over the sidewalk cracks. She slalomed behind her tight-fisted fuming friend as they turned up the walkway to the frat house.

"So what'd the loser do this time, Meg... or should I say *who* did he do?"

Meg stopped hard, pivoted, produced a pink Hello Kitty-skinned iPhone and shoved it in Whitney's face. Whitney's foot slapped the pavement and her board scraped to a halt just before her nose bumped the phone. She turned her Cali Angels hat brim-backward and blinked cross-eyed at the too-close screen.

"Hit *play*," snapped Meg. "And you'll see why his dick stayed limp last night while I sucked it through an entire episode of Desperate Housewives... and why the asshole's crotch smelled like Halloween lipstick and Twilight body spray."

Whitney poked *play* on the iPhone screen. The video commenced. The scene panned down from a reclining man's cut chest to his hardening cock, his hand wrapped around it loosely as he slowly worked its visibly growing length. A TV, hung on the wall in the background, chirped as a predatory King Sombra hungrily eyed the rear quarters of a guileless Twilight Sparkle.

"That doesn't exactly ring the opening bell of the market there, Kitten-Kat," said the guy on the screen. Whitney couldn't see his face but she knew his voice. It was Meg's long-time boyfriend, Ryan.

"Well maybe this will, you bad, bad man!" mewed a plump black-mascaraed girl in a pink lace baby doll. Her blond and pink pony tails wagged as she pounced into the scene in front of the manhandled cock. She blocked the iPhone cam's view of *My Little Pony, Friendship is Magic* afflicting both man and television.

"Kitty wants to pway wif her scratchy post! And she has a new toy for the bad man to pway wif, too!" The smirking girl on the screen turned sideways, round ass out, into a

- 135 -

feline-like pose, revealing a pretty plush black kitty tail curling out from under the edge of her pink baby doll.

"Now that's a very good kitty! C'mere, show me that new tail, and let me show Kitty what a bad man I can be."

"Promises, promises!" the girl said as she turned, pouting playfully, and stalked to the bed where Ryan was laying with his cock in his hand.

The iPhone cam followed her as she climbed up onto the bed and pawed at Ryan's cock. He teased her with it. She pretended to extend her claws and swipe at it and then suddenly lowered her head between his legs. She came up slowly, licking him with the wet tip of her tongue from the base of his balls, over his gripping fingers, to his rock hard cock head.

She paused for a mewing growl and then began lapping at the shaft and head of his cock with the flat of her tongue. Then, rearing back, she spit on the hard cock, watching the saliva drip down the head and over the foreskin before licking her small hands, cupping the head of his cock, and sliding them down, spreading the saliva down his length. With a sly smile, she opened her black painted lips and slid her mouth down onto his cock. She took almost his full length into her throat before gagging and releasing it, slick, glistening, and dripping copiously. The iPhone cam jostled as Ryan groaned and went up on his elbows for a better shot.

The girl came up to her knees with several small gags, put a black-nailed hand to her mouth, feigned innocence, and said, "Oops! Hairball!"

Ryan's head lolled back with a laugh. "Oh you are a very bad kitty!"

"Then maybe Kitty needs a spanking... or some kind of punishment around her pwetty swishy new tail!"

The plump, pink pony-tailed girl curled around and slid her round ass into Ryan's face, revealing her new black kitty tail pressed to her ass by a pair of frilly pink panties. She wiggled her hips in circles as she crouched on his chest and stomach and the tip of the plush black kitty tail brushed across Ryan's nose and mouth and chin. While his nose twitched from the swishing, he raised the phone cam to a higher angle and began rubbing the round bottom covered with pink panties, slowly tugging them down.

He must have expected the tail to slip loose as he pulled down her because he became still and gasped as he realized the tail was slipped into and held tight by her asshole. The girl giggled and wiggled her tail-sporting behind happily in his face as she looked back over her shoulder to see his look of surprise.

The girl slid her head and shoulders down next to Ryan's hard cock and nuzzled his shaft with her cheeks. He grabbed the base of the tail inserted in the girl's ass and teased and tugged on it, watching the girl's puckered asshole tremble and stretch as he slowly slid the black butt plug sporting the black plush kitty tail out. The girl arched her back and began to purr. Ryan wrapped an arm around the girl's bottom and pulled it down to his mouth. He began licking the girl's slowly closing puckered asshole while the girl mewed and sucked the man's cock.

"Um, he did not just do that," stammered Whitney.

"Um, yes, he did," snapped Meg.

"He did not just do that...with *her*."

"Oh, yes he did...with *her*."

"I'm gonna puke. What the fuck, what is she, like twelve?"

"I know, right? Imma find out how old that little Halloween hussy is and if she's a minute under eighteen this video is going to the fucking po-po! He can pucker up his own little bitch ass for his fucking cell mate!"

"Gimme that Steve Jobs brain tumor factory, girl." Whitney pried the iPhone from Meg's white-knuckled hand, gestured on the touch screen like she was casting a magic spell, and smiled as the screen revealed all she wanted and more. "Cassie Freidman, nineteen, freshman, poly-sci major, Team Edward, likes the classics: Concrete Blonde;

Nine Inch Nails; Marilyn Manson; White Zombie; into LARPing, MMOG's and WOW. And she's interested in men *and* women. She did have a sweet little muffin top... and a yummy purr... and she seems to need a big sister to help her grow up..."

"Ugh! Back off, bitch! That's the slut that's fucking my boyfriend!"

"You mean, *ex*-boyfriend! Right? Tell me this is the last fucking straw."

Finally, Whitney thought. It had been a long damned time coming.

"Not yet... not without a fucking good-bye kiss!" Meg snarled.

Whitney looked at her friend speculatively, wondering what she was up to.

"So that's why we're at Alpha Theta Tau instead of Alpha Sigma Pi on Alpha Wars Friday?" Whitney asked finally. "I wondered. So what's up, girl? You got some 'splaining to do, Lucy!"

"I don't know yet..." Meg frowned. "Just follow my lead..."

"Righteous, Fred... maybe we can use Shaggy and Scooby as bait..." Whitney rolled after Meg and picked up her board as they went inside.

Both of them had been in the Alpha Theta Tau house before. It was neat and well maintained. Not surprising for an engineering fraternity. What was surprising was the quiet. No engineers, no women, no music. But then, it was Alpha Wars night, the last battle for the year. The action would be downstairs, in the game room.

The basement door flew open and a big guy in a hoodie with a hi-tech headset, night goggles and black tactical drop leg holster rig strapped to his right blue-jeaned thigh called, "Is that you Murphy? Bout damn time! Team One is geared up and ready for insertion and you know Brody and Wang can't shoot straight without that shit they call beer! What the—! You're not Murphy!"

"Observant, there, Jason Bourne." Whitney snorted.

"Are you two from Sigma Pi? I thought they weren't sending you two 'til later, after we kick their asses? Hey, wait a minute...aren't you Killer Miller's..." The guy in the hoodie looked curiously at Meg.

"Um, yeah. I'm Ry... um, Killer Miller's girl. That's me. And this is my trusty sidekick, Lara Croft. And, yes, we're early. Killer and the boys wanted you to know what you were missing out on when they blew your asses out of cyberspace to make the world safe for free market capitalism."

"Ballsy, putting up his own woman as our victory dance prize. But whatever, as long as we get our Call of Booty after our Call of Duty. The outfits and gear are in there."

The guy in the hoodie and tactical game gear gestured to a half-open bedroom door down the hall. Just then Murphy came in with a beer keg and several cases of beer on a dolly and the guy in the hoodie jumped to help him.

"C'mon, Lara. Let's not keep the guys waiting." Meg grabbed Whitney by the arm and, with a devious smile, led her toward the bedroom.

Whitney closed the bedroom door behind them. It was dark in the frat house bedroom except for an open laptop with a *Girls, Guns and Tattoos* screen saver flashing various intensities of light as the images changed. On the roughly made double bed was a scattered pile of what looked like tactical assault gear. Meg walked to the bed and reached down into the pile.

"And just what kind of trouble are you getting us into now, Lucy? I don't think Ricky and Fred are going to be too happy." Whitney stood cross-armed by the door.

"This might get us both in the show, Ethel." Meg picked up a control panel with what looked like two hi-tech video game controls mounted on it, each with a headset. In chargers on the front of the whole assembly were two sleek black vibrators with clitoral stimulators.

"Oh no, Meg… you're not thinking what I think you're thinking! No way we're going through with this. Payback is one thing, but this? Can't you just get some guy all worked up and make the dickhead jealous, like usual?"

She was used to Meg's recklessness and red-headed passion and pride. It was what had drawn her to the girl during their freshman orientation. Whitney often wondered why Meg kept a shy, Southern Cali surfer girl and computer geek around, even if Meg had told her on many occasions that Whitney saw through her fiery exterior into her true, soft heart. Meg only ever got this furious, and this obsessed, when she was really hurt.

From the gleaming look in her eyes and the way she hurriedly began to undress, Meg was utterly devastated. Whitney knew better than to argue, stripping down to bra and panties like her friend and picking up the outfit full of straps and buckles, looking at it in confusion. Meg helped her put it on, cinching the straps with a satisfied nod and then putting on her own. Whitney helped tighten her in, admiring her friend's long, bare legs and cleavage. The gear didn't hide the way her breasts threatened to spill over the top of her Victoria's Secret bra.

Didn't hide Whitney's, either, for that matter, she noticed, adjusting her own bra straps and then picking up one of the vibrators. She hefted it, cocking her head at Meg, who held the control panel.

"Are you sure about this, Lucy?" Whitney teased. It wouldn't be the first time they'd played around together. It wouldn't even be the first time they'd played around in front of an audience. The boys loved it when they kissed each other in front of them and, Whitney admitted, she liked teasing the animals. Meg did too, in spite of her allegiances to the occasional masculine life form. Like "Killer Miller," who, she suspected, was about to get blown away by his girl. So to speak.

"We're going to give them—*and him*—the show of their lives." Meg nodded satisfactorily, using the controls to make the vibrator in Whitney's hand tremble to life.

"If you say so." Whitney heard the whoop and holler from the boys in the basement and knew their team had won. That meant they'd be expecting the show Meg was intent on giving them. But where were the girls that were supposed to be wearing these ridiculous outfits, Whitney wondered, tugging on one of the camo straps to cinch it tighter around her svelte middle.

"For me?" Meg lifted her gaze to meet her friend's and Whitney groaned. If the vibrating dildo in her hand wasn't incentive enough, those great big puppy dog eyes of Meg's were guaranteed to push her over the edge. "Pretty, pretty please?"

Meg sidled up to her, camo pressed to camo, gear jingling and jangling—how Army guys ever managed to go anywhere quietly in the stuff was beyond her—the still-buzzing vibrator pressed between their bellies now.

"With me on top?" Meg grinned, knowing and fully exploiting Whitney's weakness.

"Brat." Whitney licked her lips and swallowed, gaze falling to Meg's very pretty little mouth, longing to kiss her. And Meg looked at her like she knew it.

"Is that a yes?"

Whitney just nodded, hearing someone pounding up the stairs. It was Murphy, the chubby, bespectacled guy who had hauled in the beer keg, red-faced as he stood panting in the doorway. His eyes lit up when he saw the two of them all geared up and ready to go. Well almost. They still hadn't put on their headsets.

"We won!" Murphy exclaimed, still out of breath. "We're ready!"

"So are we." Meg waggled her eyebrows, turning the controls in her hand higher, making the vibrator hum so hard it made Whitney's hand numb. "We'll be right down."

"Yes!" Murphy grinned and didn't look in a very big hurry to go. His gaze was all over them both, up and down, back and forth, like his brain was on overload and couldn't quite decide where to settle.

"Give us two minutes." Meg waggled her fingers at him as she shut the door in his face before turning back to her friend. "Okay, once we put on the headsets, we're wired in. Ryan told me before how this works. There are little cameras right here."

Meg slipped the headset on, adjusting it amidst her red locks, and handed the other over to Whitney, who did the same.

"So we're going to be broadcasting this all over the web?" Whitney asked doubtfully.

"No, just to the other frat house. Ryan will get an eyeful in front of all his friends while he licks his wounds over his loss."

"That won't be his only loss today."

"Count on it." Meg grabbed the other vibrator and the control panel. "Let's get this party started."

Whitney followed her out the door, down the hall, both of them heading toward the sound of the guys making noise in the basement. They cheered when the girls came around the corner and Meg actually flushed, which made Whitney fall in love with her just a little bit more.

"Second thoughts?" Whitney whispered into her friend's ear. The room was full of frat boys, all of them drinking, many of them already drunk.

"Nope." Meg adjusted her head gear, looking determined as someone in the corner used the mouse to wake up a desktop, revealing the crowd of guys cat-calling. Whitney realized it was what they were both seeing—each of their cameras' view of the action.

Then the theme song to Halo started and Whitney wanted to laugh, but she didn't because Meg looked so serious.

"Let's make this good, Whit," Meg whispered, getting close and snaking her arms around her neck. Meg was warm and soft in her arms. "Remember freshman year?"

Of course she remembered. They'd put on quite a show that night. Of course, they'd both been incredibly drunk. Meg hadn't wanted to make anyone jealous that night, not exactly. She'd wanted to turn Ryan on so much he couldn't resist her. And it had worked. They'd been dating ever since, much to Whitney's chagrin. So it shouldn't have been a surprise, she supposed, that the freshman year show that had caught Ryan's attention was now being encored in order to end things between them.

Whitney had been drunk freshman year, but she wasn't drunk now. Still, she was just as determined as Meg, for the exact same reason. She didn't want Ryan anywhere near her friend again, not if she had anything to say about it. And while her intentions might not have been exactly altruistic, she did care about Meg. Way more than Ryan ever had.

"Kiss me." Meg pressed her lips to Whitney's and the guys howled, sounding like they were in pain, as Whitney's hands dropped to her friend's waist, pulling her as close as possible. The gear they were wearing was ridiculous—some nerd's fantasy, obviously—and in the way. Whitney would have to take it off as soon as possible. But first, she met Meg's kiss with a passion she wondered if her friend felt.

When they parted, Whitney felt a thick throb between her thighs. The guys were still cheering. She heard someone say, "Turn the fucking feed on! Show them what they're missing, the losers!" and knew that Ryan was seeing this. He was watching Meg and Whitney kiss on camera. And he was going to see way more than that, before the night was over.

Whitney went to her knees and the boys went from howling to silent, almost immediately, but it was all ambient noise to her. Meg smiled, looking down at her with those big green eyes, her red hair falling over her pale shoulders, and Whitney knew she could have stayed on her knees, worshipping her forever.

"A real show." Whitney whispered, nudging her nose against Meg's Hello Kitty panties. Meg made a little noise in her throat, shifting her weight, parting her thighs slightly, a sweet invitation. "You ready for this?"

"Hell yeah." Meg's eyes brightened when Whitney hooked her thumbs in her friend's panties and started sliding them down her hips. Someone let out a low whistle when they reached Meg's knees and someone else groaned like they were in pain when Whitney parted Meg's naturally curly red bush with her fingers, showing them all just how pretty her friend's pussy really was. Guys were scrambling over themselves to get a look.

And she was going to lick it, right here in front of all of them.

Her own pussy ached at the prospect. Fuck, Meg was beautiful. She couldn't blame Ryan for wanting her. Although that was the point, wasn't it? He was cheating on her, so he clearly didn't want her anymore.

But Whitney did.

"What in the hell do you two think you're doing?"

"Uh oh, Lucy." Whitney met her friend's eyes. "Sounds like Ricky's pissed."

Meg rolled her eyes, glancing over her shoulder at the screen. It was set to picture in picture. They could see the other frat, Ryan front and center, his face red with anger.

"Meg!" He bellowed. "Get the fuck out of there!"

"Make me!" she snapped, turning and showing him a very slow, deliberate middle finger. Then she turned back to her friend, running a hand through Whitney's hair. "Where were we?"

"Here." Whitney knew Ryan was going to come after them. It was only a matter of time. So she wanted to make this good. The best. Ever.

She leaned in and buried her face in Meg's pussy, hearing gasps and groans all around them. The circle of guys was getting closer, like vultures circling, looking for the spoils. But Whitney didn't have any intention of spilling a drop. She licked and sucked at Meg's clit while her friend moaned and tried to spread her thighs even wider, giving her better access.

But Whitney wanted more.

She eased Meg back, back, until the backs of her knees touched the coffee table. It was an old one, solid wood, and Whitney grabbed Meg's hips, pulling her down to sitting, following with her mouth fastened to Meg's fiery crotch the whole way.

"Oh God!" Meg cried when Whitney knelt, shoving the redhead's legs back and open wide with her hands, her tongue lapping up and down her slit.

Whitney caught a brief view of the computer screen, the camera she was wearing showing Meg's spread open pussy as Whitney's tongue delved low, dipping into the entrance of her pussy, then lower still, teasing her asshole.

"Whit!" Meg gasped. "Oh! God!"

But Whitney wanted Ryan to see it all and sat back, looking at Meg's spread open cunt, giving him a full view of what he was missing. Of what he'd given up for that stupid little kitty cat. Of what he was never going to have again, if Whitney had anything to say about it.

Then Whitney dove back in, mouth fastened on Meg's mound, using her expert tongue on her friend's sweet little clit while she worked the straps on the stupid gear they'd put on. She wanted Meg, all of her, out of this stuff. One of the guys moved to help her and she slapped his hand, giving him a dirty look. The rest of them howled and "ooooo'd!" and laughed but she didn't care. She'd marked her territory. Meg was hers.

She finally got the straps undone and Meg's bra unhooked, her breasts spilling into Whitney's waiting hands. Fuck, she was so beautiful, and she tasted so good. It was like the nectar of the gods on her tongue. Whitney couldn't get enough, sucking at her clit like a tiny little cock, swallowing her juices again and again, letting them coat her mouth and tongue.

Her own pussy felt fat, swollen, uncomfortably wet. Whitney snuck a hand down between her own thighs, shoving it under the elastic band of her panties so she could rub her own clit while she sucked on Meg's.

"Try the vibrator!" someone called. It was all a distant roar to her, but she heard that.

Whitney had forgotten about it until that moment. She picked up one of the black vibrators, recognizing the design and the controls. She had something similar, a rabbit vibrator that rotated inside with a clitoral stimulator nub that vibrated.

"Ready for this?" Whitney grinned as she slipped the cock between Meg's swollen lips, watching in fascination and utter lust as it disappeared into her flesh. Meg moaned when Whitney manipulated the controls, making the dildo rotate inside of her friend's pussy. Meg nearly came off the table when the black nub began to vibrate against her clit.

"Holy fuck!" Meg cried and there were howls and laughter around them, like jackals.

Whitney worked the vibrator in and out, teasing her friend's clit, the sound of her wet pussy being fucking filling the room. The only other sounds were Meg's moans and the heavy breathing of twenty frat boys with hard cocks. Whitney twisted and turned the humming toy, driving Meg crazy, seeing the taut tremble of her thighs. She was so fucking gorgeous, Whitney had to taste her again and used her tongue to flick the clitoral stimulator right against her little clit.

"Fuccckkkk!" Meg cried, her feet planted solidly against Whitney's shoulders. "You're going to make me fucking come!"

The hoots and hollers, the cat calls, filled the room. Whitney ignored them all, focusing on Meg's sweet button, back and forth, *flick flick flick, buzz, buzz, buzz*, determined to make her climax.

"Oh God! Now! Nowww!" Meg arched and rolled her hips, forcing Whitney to abandon the vibrator and grab on with both hands, stilling her hips and sucking her clit as Meg's pussy throbbed against her tongue. Oh she was sweet. So very sweet.

"Oh my God!" Meg sat, looking down at Whitney as the still humming vibrator dropped to the floor. Meg was dazed, breathless, and she cupped her friend's face in her hands and kissed her.

Whitney was vaguely aware of the crowd around them. Meg hadn't thought this through very well—her spontaneous, crazy, determined Meg. The guys around them grew restless. She felt the energy shift, growing hungry. They were prey in the midst of a crowd of predators. She'd known a few girls who were strippers in order to pay their college tuition and understood why it was important for there to be rules in those clubs, why they had big, burly bouncers.

For protection.

"Now you." Meg grinned, running her hands over Whitney's tits, palms brushing her nipples, making her shiver. Her voice grew louder when she said, "Bet I can make you come faster than that!"

The boys took up that gauntlet and starting laying bets, never taking their eyes off the two girls as Meg situated Whitney on the coffee table this time, sliding her panties down. Whitney looked around, knowing the guys at the other frat were seeing everything she was—the endless faces surrounding them, a bunch of drunk, horny frat boys, every single one of them with an erection he would jerk later, remembering this night.

Then she looked down at Meg as she settled herself between Whitney's parted thighs and knew Ryan was seeing this too—his girlfriend nuzzling Whitney's pussy open with her nose and tongue, their eyes locked as Whitney half-sat up on her elbows. The sight of Meg, nearly naked, straps from the gear hanging from her shoulders, kneeling between her thighs, was almost enough to send her into orbit, but it was the press of Meg's little pink tongue, slowly, softly lapping at Whitney's aching clit, that gave her the a sudden sense of flying. That, and the still slick black vibrator Meg turned on and slid into her waiting, aching cunt.

Whitney knew she should pay attention to what was going on—how the guys leaned in to watch, how they nudged each other and snickered and made comments too low for her to hear—but she couldn't concentrate, not with Meg's mouth covering her pussy, the soft quiver of her tongue so perfect, so delicious. She lost her hands in Meg's hair, rocking her hips. Meg, too, found all this stupid gear extraneous and attempted to strip her of it, but she couldn't seem to do everything at once.

One of the guys—the big one who'd met them upstairs, the one she'd called Jason Bourne—leaned over to help Meg. Whitney glared at him, brushing his hands away, trying to do the straps herself, but she couldn't reach all the fasteners.

"It's okay," he said softly, meeting her eyes. "I won't touch you."

She let him, moaning softly as Meg worked her tongue back and forth over her clit, eyes closing involuntarily. She was getting close. Oh, so close. She heard one of the guys say, "Thirty more seconds!" and knew she would make it. Meg was going to make her come that fast. Then the straps were off, her bra undone, breasts free, Meg's hand cupping and kneading them as she worked her lips and mouth and tongue between Whitney's quivering thighs. With her other hand, she fucked her senseless with the big, black vibrator.

"Ohhhh fuckkkk!" Whitney groaned, lifting her hips, completely carried away in the moment. She forgot everything except Meg, lapping studiously between her thighs, paying such nice, close attention to her clit. That focus was persistent, tenacious. She couldn't hold back anymore. "Oh! God! Meg! I'm gonna—"

And then she was. Her hips rose up high, her pussy clamping down again and again around the black cock with her climax, clit throbbing uncontrollably, a hot, sweet pulse. Meg moaned too, licking and sucking even faster, making Whitney gasp and buck on the table. She nearly fell off, but she felt hands steady her, briefly. Big hands. When she opened her eyes, she saw Jason Bourne by her side, closer than the rest.

He gave a brief nod and took a little step back.

"Damn, I want to fuck that."

Whitney heard the words and knew what was coming.

The show was over. It had to be, before things got out of control.

"Meg," Whitney said, grabbing her bra, her panties—Meg's too—when she sat. "I think we should—"

"Hold her down. I'm gonna fuck that pretty cunt."

Whitney didn't see his face. She just heard his buckle and zipper, turning her face to his crotch.

"That's not funny, man." Someone else, trying to dissuade the would-be rapist. "It's a show. It's just a show."

"You're not fucking anyone." Jason Bourne stood, putting himself between Mr. Crotch and the girls. Meg wasn't paying attention, as usual, but Whitney stood, still dizzy, and grabbed her arm, handing over her panties and bra.

"Get dressed!" Whitney hissed, yanking on her panties and quickly hooking her bra. Meg did the same, while Jason Bourne argued with a group full of drunk, horny frat boys who suddenly thought having sex with the two girls hired to put on their victory show was a brilliant idea.

Of course, they weren't the two girls that had been hired, Whitney thought. If they were, they'd have protection. And they probably only would have danced around and kissed and maybe stripped and done a few lap dances. They probably wouldn't have licked each other to climax. On a webcam.

Jesus Christ, they were stupid. Why did she let Meg talk her into these things?

"Come on, Meg."

Upstairs, there was a crash. A very loud crash. Everyone looked up toward the ceiling in surprise. The girls stopped at the bottom of the stairs and Whitney glanced behind her to see Jason Bourne following.

"Up!" He pointed at the ceiling.

Whitney started climbing, pushing Meg out ahead of her. When they got to the top, Meg opened the door.

"Meg!" Ryan roared. He was in the house, stomping down the hallway in their direction. "What in the hell are you up to?"

"I could ask you the same question!" Meg tried to peek around Jason Bourne's big frame to see her ex. Bourne had placed himself between "Killer Miller" and the girls. "Who is Cassie Friedman?"

Ryan turned white. Whitney saw him over Bourne's big, brawny shoulder.

"What are you talking about?"

"I know what you did!" Meg snapped and Whitney heard the pain in her friend's voice. "How does it feel, asshole?"

"Meg, I'm going to beat your ass black and blue!" Ryan fumed.

"You're not going to touch anyone!" Whitney growled, trying to push her way past Bourne, who turned and grabbed her shoulders with a sigh.

"Let me handle this." Bourne turned toward Ryan, putting the flat of his hand against his chest and pushing hard enough Ryan found himself upended. He fell hard on his ass, making Meg laugh in delight.

"No one is touching anyone." Bourne blocked Ryan as he tried to get up, waving the girls on by. "And if you even think about it, Miller, you're going to be the one who's black and blue."

"Fuck you!" Ryan tried to get up but Bourne stepped on his hand, palm flat on the floor, and he howled in pain.

"Come on!" Whitney edged past Bourne, pulling Meg with her, heading down the hallway to the room they'd originally geared up in.

"He's such an asshole!" Meg mumbled as they started getting dressed.

"I told you that a long time ago." Whitney didn't like saying she told her so. But she had. Several times.

"Well at least I got him back." Meg pulled her t-shirt over her head. "Now he knows what it feels like to be cheated on."

"Let Cassie Friedman have him." Whitney zipped her jeans. "They deserve each other."

She peeked out the door and saw Bourne and Killer Miller in heated argument. She wanted to get them the hell out of there. They'd go back to their little apartment, eat Ben & Jerry's, watch Breaking Bad reruns and she'd let Meg cry on her shoulder. Because she knew that was coming. Any minute, that was coming. Meg was like a dam, holding everything back, until she couldn't anymore.

"Whit...?"

"Huh?" Whitney tried to judge if Ryan would notice them sneaking down the hall and out the front door.

"Thanks." Meg's arms went around her waist, her cheek resting against Whitney's shoulder. "You're so good to me."

"I know." Whitney smiled, leaning her cheek against the door jamb.

"Too good." Meg swallowed. The sound was loud in the quiet room. "You know I love you, right?"

"Right." Whitney felt her throat closing up, tears stinging her eyes. Damnit, she didn't have time for this. "Love you too, sis."

Love you like a sister. They'd uttered those words since freshman year, Whitney lying through her teeth, because she didn't love her like a sister, not at all. She loved her, plain and simple. And she knew she was never, ever going to have her, unless it was like this, as one of Meg's little schemes.

"No." Meg turned Whitney to her, eyes soft. "I mean… I love you, Whit. I love you. Not like a sister. Like…"

"Meg…" Now it was Whitney's turn to swallow.

"I've been really stupid, for a really long time," Meg admitted. "Do you even still want me?"

"More than anything." Whitney's heart soared.

"Let's go home."

Their lips met and everything else disappeared.

Then a cheer went up from somewhere down in the basement. It wasn't until that moment that Whitney realized they were still wearing their head gear. They were still broadcasting everything.

Whitney laughed, pulling it off and tossing it on the bed and Meg did the same.

"Come on."

"Thanks!" Whitney mouthed, waving to Bourne as they snuck past. It wasn't fast enough though because Ryan glimpsed them.

"You fucking dyke!" He screamed at Whitney.

"Shut up, asshole!" Meg gave him the finger. "I hope she scratches your eyes out!"

"Fuck you!" He snapped, pinned to the wall by Bourne's big arms. "You two deserve each other!"

"We do." Meg smiled and put her arm around her best friend and new lover.

On their way out the door, they ran into two girls coming up the walkway.

"Is this Alpha Theta Tau?" the tall blonde asked. "We're supposed to do a show."

Meg and Whitney looked at each other and burst out laughing.

Stay

I knew Isaac was dying. He was limping now, his left leg following him slowly and pathetically whenever he was forced by hunger or some other bodily function to make his way toward some physical peace. He was dying, and I hated watching, but I couldn't let him go. He still slept in my bed every night, his body big and warm next to mine, even his snores a comfort. When he started coughing, I took him in again. They said he had pneumonia, and they gave me more medication and told me to say my goodbyes, because they didn't think it would be much longer.

They were wrong. I had stroked his head in my lap while he coughed and wheezed, and my tears fell onto him in the darkness. A few times, he had stopped and I thought, *Oh my God, this is really it!* Then he had drawn another breath—a harsh, raw sound—but there it was, and he was still with me.

Isaac liked to follow me around the house, although it was obviously painful for him, so I tried to stay in one place when I came home at night. Work had become a nightmare. I spent eight hours worrying that he was in pain; that I was going to come home and find him gone.

I wanted to be there at the end. I wanted him to remember my hand stroking his graying chin, my voice singing to him, even if it was choked with hot tears.

When my sister called, the obligatory weekly call, I could hear her children arguing in the background.

"You need to let him go, Claire. What you really need to do is sell the house altogether and move on. Get a little apartment somewhere. Start dating again. Seriously."

I knew that she wanted to help. I thanked her politely for her advice, changed the subject, and listened to her ramble on about her life, her job, her husband, her kids. Then, I would go snuggle in bed with Isaac.

There was just nothing else I wanted to do more.

Of course, that wasn't entirely true. Even I knew that.

* * * *

"Isaac?" My voice was panicked already.

He hadn't been at the door when I unlocked it and stumbled in with groceries. He wasn't lying on the couch, or even in front of it, a spot he was settling for now that he couldn't manage the painful step up without my help. I tossed the groceries on the kitchen counter, my purse and briefcase forgotten in front of the open door, my keys still swinging from the lock.

"Isaac?" I called, more loudly now, listening for the lumbering, lopsided sound of him climbing off the bed and down the stairs. Nothing.

"Isaac?" I was nearly screaming as I took the stairs two at a time. I looked in my room first. He wasn't on the bed. He wasn't next to it.

I flew through each room, calling him. The silence was choking me. I couldn't understand where he could possibly be. I was still in heels, and nearly twisted my ankle coming down the stairs. I steadied myself with the handrail, and tossed my shoes off, heading toward the kitchen in my nylons. I surveyed the kitchen. Nothing out of place.

Then I heard something—a faint yelp. I noticed the basement door was slightly ajar, and I knew.

"Isaac!" I cried, throwing the door open wide, and there he was at the bottom of the stairs. I couldn't tell how badly he was hurt, but he was alive. He lifted his head to look up at me. I was strangely grateful for that.

I grabbed a thick, heavy bath towel and ran to gather him up. This was never easy, even now, when he weighed half as much as he used to. He still weighed enough to make me strain and grunt as I picked him up. He whined and cried but let me lift him and carry him to the car.

I remembered my purse and my keys, but I left my shoes and remembered them only when I was sitting in the waiting room and saw that my feet were filthy and my nylons had holes in the toes.

* * * *

"Claire, I want to put him down."

I was stubbornly shaking my head before the woman had even finished her sentence. This new vet had kind eyes, and there was such sympathy in them that I had to look away. This couldn't be happening.

I wished Matthew were here. Matthew would have pursed his lips into a thin white line, written a prescription on his pad and sent us home. There were no broken bones, after all, although this new vet seemed to think Isaac might have suffered another "doggie stroke," which may have caused the fall.

"Listen, doc..." I started, then stopped, unable to approximate anything close to what I was feeling in the moment, or to offer any explanation, let alone an impossible decision.

"Call me Mary," the vet urged. I wasn't really hearing her. My focus was on Isaac.

"I shouldn't have left the door open. I don't know what I was thinking," I blurted, reaching a trembling hand out to stroke Isaac's thick red coat. He was panting on the table, his pink tongue lolling onto the metal surface, leaving a pool of saliva.

"This isn't about a fall, Claire," she said. "This dog is fifteen years old. He's had three vestibular incidents—"

"That he's recovered from," I interjected. Those were the "doggie strokes," although unlike human strokes, they weren't blood clots, but had something to do with miscommunication between the brain and inner ear.

"Yes," Mary went on. "To a degree... but you know he still has a great difficulty walking. He also has a very large tumor on his left haunch here that we know is cancerous, and he's blind in one eye."

Stupid! I berated myself. Leaving the basement door open. What was I thinking?

"This old guy has lived a great life, but he's in a lot of pain now... really, a lot of pain," she emphasized, and I turned my head, closing my eyes for a moment.

"We need to think about what's best for him." Mary patted Isaac on the back, and I noticed the slight wince he made, although he accepted the affection readily enough.

I looked miserably at Isaac, and when I slid my hand up to his head to scratch behind his floppy ears, he looked up at me with such love and trust and sheer adoration that I felt nauseous.

Mary dipped her head, trying to catch my eye, but I evaded her. She sighed, leaning back on the table, and stroked the dog's fur. The silence stretched and became more brittle. I knew the vet was angry at me, that she somehow felt that I was being selfish and irresponsible. I didn't know how to explain it to her, so I said nothing, and just continued to pet Isaac like he was the only living thing in the room.

"Listen, I know this is a hard decision," Mary said. Her voice never lost that softness, and in that moment, I hated her for it. Mary's hand edged close to mine in the dog's fur, and brushed over it lightly, pressing gently before moving on. "I'm not asking you to make it today, but I would like you to think about it. Would you do that?"

"Please," I said shakily. "You just don't understand."

"I do," Mary assured me, touching my hand again. The warmth startled me, both in her hands and her voice, and I looked up at her. Mary's eyes were trying to tell me something, but I didn't know what. "It's okay, Claire. You can take him home. Keep him on the medications he's on, he'll be... well, the same as he's been, I imagine."

"Thank you," I breathed. I smiled through tears at Isaac.

"Come on, big man, let's get you home."

She helped, in spite of my protest, get Isaac settled in the front seat of my car. We stood there for a moment on the gravel drive, and I looked across the street past the wrought iron gates where the sun was just beginning to sink behind trees and headstones while Mary tucked her thick dark curls behind her ears against the wind and watched.

I found it surprising, in spite of the fact I'd been coming here since Isaac was just a puppy, that this place was right across from the cemetery. Somehow, I never noticed before. Maybe I'd just never had a reason to pay attention. My stomach clenched.

Reaching for Mary's hand, I squeezed it and gave her a sad, apologetic little smile. "Well, thank you," I said, clearing my throat. "Thanks for helping Isaac. I've got to get going."

"Listen, I want to tell you something." Mary leaned in to touch my arm to keep me from opening the driver's side door when I let go of her hand. I looked down at the hand on my arm and then up at her, unsure. "I know you love him, but he's suffering, Claire. You need to let him go." She pressed me, her words, her hand on my arm. I bit my lip, and then looked down at the keys in my hand, fumbling for the right one.

"I can't," I choked out, shaking her arm off and unlocking door. Mary let me go, stepping back away from the car as the tires crunched the gravel underneath.

"No, no, no..." I breathed, one hand in Isaac's fur, the other on the steering wheel. I glanced up, and my rear view mirror revealed Mary still standing there, hands in her coat pockets, watching me as I pulled away.

* * * *

It amazed me that the dream was almost always the same—although it had probably been a year since the last. It was always so real, so like the way it had really happened. I could remember Jack's face, how pallid and thin, absolutely motionless. I would believe him dead already, except for the steady beat of the breathing tube going into the hole in his throat.

I watched that pulse with all the force of my being, willing him to live, wanting him to sit up and smile at me again, just one more time, knowing that every breath was a miracle and held only one thing now—hope. There was only me and Jack and the steady beat of his heart.

Then there was a flurry of activity, talk of living wills and signing papers, and tubes being removed, and then as I watched, that heart that had held for me everything I knew in the world, every secret, every quiet, tender moment, simply stopped beating, and he was gone.

Isaac howled every time I woke up gasping from this dream.

In the beginning, I had, too, burying my hot, wet face in his fur and howling with him, sobbing and sobbing until I thought we might end up broken things, unfixable. Over the past couple years, I had grown used to the dream in the ways I had grown used to life without Jack, in ways I never thought possible.

Tonight, I woke up breathless and shrieking, my hands at my throat, always at my throat, as if I could give him my breath somehow, even now. Isaac was next to me—I could feel the weight of him in the bed.

The digital clock read 2:28 a.m. I leaned back on my arms, letting my head fall forward, waiting for the physical transition from dream to consciousness. It was slow in coming, and made me tingle, like blood beginning to flow into a limb that had been deeply asleep.

It was only then that I realized that I hadn't woken Isaac.

Poor guy—he'd had a rough few weeks since his fall down the stairs. I slid my hand over his silky back and curled myself around him, aching for warmth. He didn't stir. I sat straight up in bed, the intuition and realization hitting with a horrific force. I fumbled for the lamp, but I didn't really need to.

I already knew.

* * * *

Mary's voice was clear, almost as if she'd already been awake at this late hour.

"Dr... Mary...?" I whispered into the phone. The vet's pager number, in case of emergencies, was stuck to the refrigerator with a Betty Boop magnet, and I stood, still bed-warm and shivering in my t-shirt, peering at it by the dim light of the stove hood.

"Yes, this is Dr. Rennalls. Is there an emergency?" Her voice was even stronger now, and I could tell the difference between them, now and a moment ago. I had woken her.

"Isaac," I said, my voice rising a little, trying not to be panicked. "Something's really wrong."

"Claire?" Her voice changed again, somehow, her tone softer. "What is it?"

"I... I don't know. I woke up from a bad dream. He didn't wake up. He won't wake up!" I began sobbing. Turning my back to the fridge, I leaned on it for support and found myself sliding down onto the linoleum, raking a large collection of magnets and papers down with me.

"Claire, Claire," she murmured. "It's okay, hang on. I'll be right over, give me ten minutes."

* * * *

I had forgotten to lock the door, and after a few minutes of knocking, Mary finally just let herself in. She found me there, in front of the refrigerator, hugging my t-shirt around my knees and rocking gently.

"Where is he, Claire?" she asked, touching my arm, my shoulder, trying to find the right point of contact. Finally, I saw her and reached for her, pressing my hot face into the cool skin of her throat.

"In my room," I finally managed.

Mary nodded, but didn't move. It was then that I began to sob, and she simply held me. I was making small hitching noises when I wiped at my eyes, embarrassed now, pushing at her. Mary let me push her away, searching my face before standing and holding out her hand. I accepted it and stood, allowing her support.

"Sit here." She guided me to one of the backless kitchen chairs. "I'll be right back."

I watched her disappear down the dark hallway. My eyes closed, and I rested my head on my arms. The moment

I did, I saw Isaac chasing Andre, Jack throwing the graying tennis ball named after the graying tennis star.

It never mattered where Andre landed, Isaac would hunt him out and bring him back, leaving a sopping wet ball at our feet. It was my least favorite game for this reason, my bare toes often the victim of cold, unwelcome, slobbery wetness, but it was Isaac's, and thankfully, Jack's, favorite. Jack would spend hours out on the patio reading the paper or on his laptop, tossing while Isaac fetched. It was almost a meditation—*toss, fetch, toss, fetch.* Jack could talk on his cell, type, and still manage to pitch Andre halfway across our yard for Isaac to clamber after.

I couldn't hear anything from down the hall, although I was really listening hard.

I remembered that one of Jack's distracted throws had managed to make it over the fence, and Isaac, determined, had scaled it. He'd snagged Andre like some outfielder in a hurry, never seeing the car heading toward him in the middle of our street.

We were both standing—I remembered how my hand went to my throat. Isaac had met us back at the fence, Andre secured in his jaws, unaware of any danger, just looking over at us like, "Hey, let me back in, I want to play!" That had really been a close one.

This is just a close one, a voice whispered. He's had them before. He's going to be okay. It was a mantra I had repeated again and again at Jack's bedside. He's going to be okay, he's going to be okay. Except he wasn't.

"He's not dead, Claire." Mary's voice, incredulous, lifted my head and my spirits. "I think it's another vestibular incident, probably his last. His respiration and heart rate are very low."

The question hung there, unasked.

"You'll take him in?" I asked.

Mary closed her eyes, nodded. "Yes." Defeated, Mary said, "I'll drive."

I smiled, standing to follow her toward the front door. Mary stopped me, her eyes dipping down to my bare legs below my t-shirt.

"You might want to get dressed. I'll get Isaac to the car."

"Oh."

I fumbled through my drawers for a pair of sweats while Mary carefully collected the dog. I found an old pair of Jack's, way too long, but the waist tied. I found myself sobbing again as I pulled them on, missing the left leg hole three times before Mary was back at my elbow, guiding me. I let myself lean on her.

* * * *

"He's resting comfortably. It's all I can do for him now, Claire. Let me take you home," Mary urged, her hand reaching to cover mine, clutching the bars of the cage.

"Can't I stay here?" I asked. Mary opened her mouth to respond and then saw my eyes and closed it again. "I don't want to be alone tonight."

Mary stood there for a moment, her eyes searching my face.

"We can't stay here," she said. "But you can come home with me if you want. We'll check on him in the morning."

I shook my head, looking down, following the pattern in the tile with my eyes. "I couldn't. I don't want to disturb you. No, I'll go home. I'll—" my voice trailed off as my eyes got caught in a swirl, around and around, on the floor.

Mary's hand slid around my shoulder as she steered me toward the door. "I'll drive you home then, okay?"

The night was cool, and I shivered in my seat, even when Mary turned up the heat. I splayed my fingers against the vent in an attempt to warm them. I often got cold this way when I was upset, as if my body was conserving its energy, drawing the blood in from my limbs into my core, deep into my heart, where I needed it most. I remembered wearing layers of clothes at the hospital and still sitting there shivering night after night.

"So, where is your husband?" Mary asked me.

I started. "My husband?"

"Your ring," Mary said, pulling the car out of the parking lot.

There was no traffic on the roads, I noticed, and I watched as the trees passed by the windows like ghosts.

I pulled my hands away from the vent, looking at my wedding ring, and replied, "He's dead."

A silence stretched between us, and I leaned back against the headrest, hugging myself, although the car was warm now.

"I'm sorry," she murmured, a hand briefly rubbing my arm.

"I shouldn't wear it anymore," I said, closing my eyes. The heat had started to reach my limbs, relaxing me a little bit. "It's been two years. It just keeps the weirdoes at bay, you know?"

She didn't respond, and I dozed to the rumble of the engine and the rolling of the wheels on the pavement. When I woke, my forehead was leaning against the window, my breath fogging the glass. The car had stopped moving. I used my hand to clear the haze, but I wasn't looking at my house.

"Where—?"

"My place," she said, cutting the engine and pocketing her keys. "Come on in with me, Claire. I have a spare room. There's no reason you need to be alone tonight."

I felt tears stinging my eyes. I was too exhausted to argue. It had been a long time since someone had been this kind to me. Maybe since those first months after Jack had died. I followed Mary into the house, looking around but unable to really take in my surroundings. I felt numb.

"What about you?" I asked as she shrugged off her coat. "Husband, boyfriend?"

"Girlfriend," she said, the hangers inside the hall closet tinkling together as she hung up her coat. "But not anymore. Do you want something? Warm milk, hot chocolate, something to help you sleep?"

I shook my head, unfazed by Mary's revelation, still hugging myself as I stood in the foyer. Mary came over, her eyes searching as she unbuttoned my coat for me, helping me take it off and hanging it in the closet next to her own.

"Come on, then." She took my hand and led me upstairs.

"Nice," I commented, sitting on the double bed and looking around the room. I was only seeing the outlines of things, as if the world had been bled of its color. I remembered this feeling but had never expected it to come again after what happened with Jack.

She went to the door, turning to say, "My room is right next door. Bathroom is down the hall, first door on the left."

"Thanks." I stared at the wall, the flowered wallpaper catching my attention. I followed the pattern with my eyes. I remembered counting blind slats in Jack's hospital room— anything to distract myself.

Mary closed the door, and I lay back on the bed. It was soft, like lying on a cloud, very different from the firm— almost hard—mattress I had once shared with Jack. My eyes closed and I saw him, tilting up my chin for a casual kiss goodbye, patting Isaac on the head before he headed off to work. I hadn't had memories like this for years. It felt like some dam had burst inside of my head.

I pulled off my sweats, wiggling under the comforter and turning out the light. I found my body responding to the softness of the mattress and the lateness of the hour. I drifted, not realizing that I was crying until the pillow became so wet I had to turn it over.

The dream was the same—it was always the same. I kissed his forehead, and he was still warm, but he was gone away somewhere I couldn't reach him anymore. The weight in my chest made me feel as if I was drowning, gasping for breath. I woke and grasped the comforter in my hands, searching for Isaac, still disoriented and half-asleep.

At first, I didn't know where I was, and then I remembered. Isaac was at the vet's. I was in Mary's spare room. I looked at the clock on the night stand and saw that only an hour had passed. I closed my eyes, trying to will myself back to sleep. I heard something in the hallway, and the door opened.

"Claire?" It was Mary, whispering. "Are you okay?"

"Yeah," I whispered back.

"You were crying," Mary said. "Are you sure?"

"I was?" I put my hands to my cheeks. They were damp. "I'm sorry. I didn't mean to wake you."

"I just wanted to make sure you were okay..."

"I guess," I replied, drawing a shaky breath and staring up at the ceiling. "How do we define okay?"

"Well... goodnight." Mary went to close the door.

"Wait." The light spilling in from the hallway was inviting, and Mary's presence was comforting. "Will you stay?

Mary moved toward the bed, sitting on the edge. She was wearing a long t-shirt, I noticed. Her hand moved in my hair, pushing it out of my eyes. "Just feel like you want some company?"

"Yes."

I moved over and let her slip in beside me. We laid there in the darkness for a while, listening to each other breathe. My heart was beating fast, and I didn't know why. I slid my feet over to touch hers. Mine were cold.

"He was Jack's dog," I whispered. She didn't answer, but I heard her breathing change. She'd heard me. She was listening. "He was my dog, too, but you know how some dogs just kind of choose someone to love more than anyone else? Jack was that person for Isaac."

"Yes," Mary said, her voice and her feet warming me.

"Jack was that person for me, too," I whispered, feeling tears stinging my eyes. I couldn't talk for a while around the lump in my throat. I was remembering Isaac as a puppy, tumbling and loping after us in the mornings, always underfoot. He would lay on Jack's feet while he made eggs or loaded the dishwasher. I remembered how he never got mad—he would just step over the little red curled-up bundle. Of course, when Isaac was a hulking sixty pound dog, he did the same thing, curling up on our feet like he thought he was just a little pup. Jack still patiently stepped over him. I smiled through my tears.

"It's hard to let go," Mary said after a while. "People want to hang on to the things they love. It's only natural."

"Oh, God," I breathed. "Please don't give me the 'he's in a better place' speech."

"I don't know if it's better," Mary said. "I don't even know if it's different. I don't know. I wish I did. That moment when a soul leaves... It's so clear, that moment. One minute, the person you love is there, and the next minute, they're not."

I nodded, feeling tears slipping down my temples. I remembered watching Jack's face, hearing his breath, knowing he was still there. It didn't matter what they said, that he was as good as dead, would be a vegetable—I could still feel him.

Whatever part of him that made him Jack was still there. And then it wasn't.

"What happens between one minute and the next? Is it the body running down, like a clock unwinding? I just don't know." Mary sighed in the dark, and she slid her hand across the mattress to touch mine. "What do you think?"

The lump was back again in my throat. I remembered my sister explaining Jack's death to her children, how her words had made my jaw clench, my eyes burn. "He's in a better place. His body is gone, but his spirit is all around us, all the time." I'd had such an overwhelming urge to punch something when she said that—and then she said the words, "God knows best. It's his plan." My heart still ached with the heaviness of those.

"I think this is it," I replied, my voice trembling. I heard it and it didn't even sound like my own. "I think this is all we'll have—all we'll ever have. When I lost Jack, I lost him. Forever. There's no bringing him back. I hold on so tightly to Isaac because..."

"Because he's all you have," Mary murmured, and I nodded, a shuddering sigh turning into real tears. "It's okay to hold on, Claire. Loving isn't just about letting go. It's about holding sometimes, too."

I sobbed, turning to her in the dark, whispering, "Hold me. Please." She did, her hand stroking my hair, and I could feel small kisses falling on the top of my head. Her body was warm and soft, yielding to me as I wept against her shirt, twisting it in my hands, mimicking the sensation in my gut, something knotted and churning.

She let me cry until I was floating on my feelings like riding waves, up and down. My cheeks burned, my eyes felt swollen shut, but I felt cleansed somehow, like the morning after a hard summer rain. I rested against her, and we were silent except for an occasional hitching sigh.

I became aware of the warmth of us together, her sweet breath on my cheek. Her heart was a reminder, a constant lubdub under my ear. I remembered laying my head against Jack's chest like this when he was sick, hearing that sound. It was the sound of life. I reveled in it.

I turned my face up to hers, seeing just the outline of her cheek, the glimmer of her eyes. It had been so long since anyone had touched me or had seen so directly into my heart. I stroked her cheek. "Thank you."

"Claire—" she whispered my name like she wanted to say something, but nothing followed, and then I was kissing her, surprised at and lost in her softness and warmth. Her hand stroked me, my hair, my shoulder, my breast, my belly. It was a tender thing, like our kiss, stretching on and on. I let out a shuddering breath against her neck, pressing myself into her, wanting to be closer.

"Listen," Mary whispered, and I noticed that her breath was coming faster, like mine. "I don't think we should be doing this."

"I'm tired of *should*," I told her, sliding my thigh up between hers. "I'm tired of *supposed to*, I'm tired of *have to*,

I'm just... I'm just so tired of closing my eyes so tight all the time."

Her face was inches from mine, and I could feel how taut her muscles were, as if she were holding something back. I wanted it. I wanted everything, all at once, and I wanted it now. I wanted to take and to have—and to hold. Definitely to hold.

"Claire, we—" I pressed my fingers to her lips, and then I pressed my lips there, too.

"I want you to help me," I whispered as I slipped my arms around her. "You said you wanted to help me. You brought me home so you could help me. I'm asking you to help me."

"How?" she asked, holding onto me.

"Just... just make me feel alive again," I whispered, my hands seeking her warmest, softest places in the dark. She gasped and sighed when I touched her, and I felt her longing. I hadn't felt so close to someone in so long. "Please. Touch me. Make me feel."

I don't know if it was my words or my hand rocking between her legs that convinced her, but I felt her give into it, into me, moaning softly against my mouth and kissing me, long and deep. Her tongue moved in a slow exploration as she rolled over me, the heat of her body against mine a warm shock. She kissed my throat, my collarbone, her mouth moving downward while her hands pressed my shirt up.

I closed my eyes and let her, helping her remove my shirt, tugging and pulling at hers until she took it off. When our panties were tangled up on the floor, the feel of her skin against mine reminded me immediately that I had a body, that my body was as hungry for touch as my soul was for answers. I couldn't find answers, no matter how long or how hard I looked, but I could satisfy this craving.

Everything about us together was impossibly comfortable and soothing and right in that moment. My mind wasn't racing, it was floating. My body wasn't trembling with the fear of loss, but instead it was quivering with anticipation. It had been a long time since I had looked forward to anything. When Mary's mouth reached my navel, she stopped and rested her cheek there against my belly that lifted her with its gentle rise and fall.

"Claire, are you sure?" she asked after a moment, her hand gently stroking the sensitive skin of my inner thigh.

"I feel like I'm dying, too," I whispered. My hands were in her hair, pressing her downward. "Every day the sun comes up feels like another betrayal. Please." My hands insisted, and I wiggled my body upward on the bed, helping her between my thighs. I wanted to spread myself as wide as the Earth for her, trembling and vulnerable and completely open.

Her tongue brought tears to my eyes, but for the first time since I could remember, they weren't tears of sorrow. I let them slip down my temples, losing myself in the sweetness of her mouth moving against me. She kissed my pussy like she kissed my mouth, a kind and tender exploration. It felt like a gift she was giving me, and my body responded in gratitude, riding a gently swelling wave toward a distant shore. She was carrying me with her somehow, pressing me onward.

It was like I was floating, but I was resting on her or in her or with her. Maybe it was just that I became her, the soft sounds of my pleasure washing over us both. Nothing had ever felt so good or so right. She found the sensitive hood of my clit, pushing it back with her tongue again and again. I gasped and clutched at her hair, rocking with her. I felt her hands moving over my hips, cupping my ass, guiding me against her willing mouth.

I wanted it to go on forever, such exquisite torture, my body racing to catch up to something but never quite reaching it. Mary was helping me get there, her mouth a steady, insistent encouragement, the sensation taking me with it now, instead of me trying to follow. I cried out at the moment of that swift, pulsing release, feeling completely undone. The flutter of my muscles was a delicious reminder, a tightening and a letting go, again and again and again.

Mary stayed between my legs, resting her cheek against my thigh, her whole hand cupping my mound, as if she could hold me in, but I flowed out around her fingers, a glorious emancipation dripping over my flesh. She came up to me after a while, kissing her way, making me shiver with the delightful sensation, as if my body had been numb and was now coming, buzzing and tingling, to life.

I rolled to her and we lay there, pressed belly to belly. We didn't have to speak. I closed my eyes and we listened to each other breathe, drifting off together. It was the first time since Jack had died that I felt any sense of real peace, as if I had died into my own life somehow and had been reborn. It was too big for words, and I felt her knowing it as she pulled my belly to hers, and we twined ourselves together in the dark.

* * * *

It was full morning when I woke, and Mary was gone, the indentation of her head still on the pillow next to mine. The door was open a crack, and I could hear her moving around downstairs, and I could smell eggs cooking. I thought that's what might have actually woken me. I was starving.

I was sitting on the bed, pulling on my t-shirt, eager to go downstairs, when the phone rang. There was one sitting on the night table next to the bed, and I watched it ringing, knowing who it was.

Mary answered it, and her voice carried up the stairs. I could hear her clearly. "Yes, I brought him in last night. It was an emergency—" She was listening. I could feel the silence. "Okay, thanks."

I didn't move, I didn't think, I didn't talk, I didn't breathe.

When I looked up, she was standing in the doorway.

"Isaac—" she said.

"I know." My eyes were full of tears when I looked at her, but my heart was full of some strange combination of sorrowful joy. I didn't understand it.

"I'm sorry," she said, and I saw the gift she had given me in her eyes. It was still there, like a light shining over my face as I looked at her.

"It'll be okay," I said, holding out my hand to her. And it was.

ABOUT SELENA KITT

Selena Kitt is a New York Times and USA Today bestselling and award-winning author of erotic fiction. She is one of the highest selling erotic writers in the business. With over a million books sold, she is the cream-at-the-top of erotica!

Her writing embodies everything from the spicy to the scandalous, but watch out-this kitty also has sharp claws and her stories often include intriguing edges and twists that take readers to new, thought-provoking depths.

When she's not pawing away at her keyboard, Selena runs an innovative publishing company (www. excessica.com) and in her spare time, she devotes herself to her family—a husband and four children—and her growing organic garden. She also loves bellydancing and photography.

Her books *EcoErotica* (2009), *The Real Mother Goose* (2010) and *Heidi and the Kaiser* (2011) were all Epic Award Finalists. Her only gay male romance, *Second Chance*, won the Epic Award in Erotica in 2011. Her story, *Connections*, was one of the runners-up for the 2006 Rauxa Prize, given annually to an erotic short story of "exceptional literary quality," out of over 1,000 nominees, where awards are judged by a select jury and all entries are read "blind" (without author's name available.)

She can be reached on her website at:

www.selenakitt.com

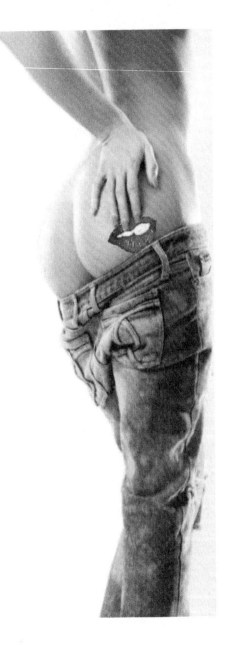

Made in the USA
Monee, IL
19 July 2023

39591213R00104